S0-BIN-510

FADED
LOVE

Faded Love

By Josephine Cunnington Edwards

Illustrated by Fred Collins

Review and Herald® Publishing Association
Washington, DC 20039-0555
Hagerstown, MD 21740

Copyright © 1961 and 1989 by the
Review and Herald® Publishing Association
Library of Congress Card Number 61-11982

PRINTED IN THE U.S.A.

Faded LOVE

EMIL, FOLLOWING the plow, could almost hear the chains clank about his ankles. Around stumps, over hills and rises of ground, he guided the iron-tipped wooden plowshare in the grueling toil of breaking up new land for pa. Yes, for pa, though he never had a word of commendation for work well done, or a smile or a pleasantry of any kind.

"A slave, I am," he would mutter, and gaze off at the landscape in the depth of his misery. For no matter what he did, he could not please his father, who ruled his whole household with an unloving and iron hand.

Mother, loving and good, had never been able to call her soul her own. Father decided everything. He told her what to do and when to do it, even the day when she should make the candles, and when to leach the lye from the wood ashes for the making of soap, and when she should begin to dry the apples. He was always loud and faultfinding, as if it were soft and weak to be kind, and might lessen the harsh authority he held over his wife and children. His severity was hard. It was worse than hard; it was galling slavery.

They had all come over from the fatherland, when Emil, the oldest, was just an apple-cheeked lad in bulky Old World clothes. He remembered Castle Garden, where he had been taken with his father by a man who said he would show them the sights of the city for a dollar. It had once been the place where immigrants came, but his father's family had gotten off at Ellis Island. The great round building had been everything since its construction in 1808—a fort, a cabaret, a music and dance hall, and an immigrant clearinghouse. LaFayette had been entertained at a great reception there, and in 1850 Phineas T. Barnum had gathered an audience of more than ten thousand to hear Jenny Lind, the Swedish nightingale.

He remembered the hotel where the family had stayed briefly, before father had found passage up the Hudson River to the land for which he had negotiated long before they had embarked for America on the creaking sailing ship.

P. T. Barnum had a wonderful museum down on Broadway and Paulina streets. A milling crowd of people gathered there every day, and folks told his father it was one of the wonder spots in New York. As Emil recalled the occasion, a black bitterness welled up within him. He, and even ma, had been so curious. The great painted signs and pictures out in front had made even his mother brighten with brief curiosity. Emil understood, young as he was, that she would have liked so well to go in and see some of the marvels that Barnum had gaudily adverti~d out in front. But father had decided for all of them.

"We don't spend moneys for nothings," he had decreed loudly. It was always so.

And even on the homestead and in the arranging of the house—in every decision, great and small—father had to have the first and the last voice, until Emil wondered how his mother could live at all in the harshness of her narrow life. He was young and could someday escape; but she, never. He knew that if there were spareribs and smearcase and sauerkraut for dinner, or if there was to be coffee kuchen, it was because his father had told his mother what to make, just how to make it, when to start, and when it should be done.

One thing about father, Emil thought gratefully, he *did* come to America. And his logic about coming was the only thing with which Emil had concurred most heartily. He had said more than once in his high, harsh, faultfinding voice:

"To live in Europe—yes, even in the fatherland—is no chance for a man who wants to get ahead. Yah, every kaiser and every czar and every king thinks he had better have a war so as to make his name big in the history books and in his country. And the farm boys and the shop boys and even the beggars and servants and students are sown like seeds that will never spring up and bear fruit, except for another war worse than the last one. We came to this new country to get as far as we can from the fights of Germany and France and Austria—yes, and the others too."

Yes, it was the one thing that his father said to which Emil could agree, even feverishly.

His mother had her pride, even if she was so humble and so subservient to father. In their rare moments alone with each other she used to recount the exploits of her family with prideful remembering.

OUR FAMILY, they were important people in the old country. My father—in school he won a prize for scholarship, and the kaiser himself visited the school and gave it to him. He was given free schooling to be a Lutheran minister. But no—he did not like that. He went to school, but soon he had to go into the army, for the German army gets them all. About the time that Hans and I were married, my parents came here to America and opened a dressmaking shop on Manhattan. Father had the first sewing machine in that part of town. Later the people came and tried to wreck his shop. They said the new machine was spoiling the work of the hand workers and bringing more poverty on the poor."

"Mother," Emil asked, "why is it that people fight progress? We now know that the sewing machine in industry has helped the poor as much as it has helped anyone. It has enabled even the poor to make good clothing at home and in only a fraction of the time."

"Yah, and even your father fights the new things," his mother commented, not complainingly but merely stating a fact. "He is always saying that what was good enough for his father and his mother is good enough for us."

Emil nodded, remembering times without number when he had read of a better way of doing some farm chore, in some agriculture weekly or in the newspaper. He remembered that old Hans would shout him down if he would so much as suggest it. It took the heart out of him.

None of the neighbors had any use for the old man, Hans Huener. He was forceful and quarrelsome, and inclined to try to force his opinion on every person who spoke to him. He was avoided because of his ugly temper. It isolated the family and gave Helga Huener no neighbors, such as afford pleasure for most women. He said that he would rather see ma dead than to have her chasing around with the buggy and driving to town at all hours like some of the worthless neighbor women were doing. So poor ma seldom got out of her own dooryard.

The only time Emil saw his mother brighten and look relaxed was when old Hans was away from the house for the day or when he went to town. Then she would get the girls to come in from the garden and the dairy, and they would make kuchen and brew a pot of coffee, and sit and laugh and talk in an animation that Hans would have been surprised to see should he happen to walk in on them. Martha and Huldah got work as soon as they could, and both of them married young and moved out of the county. It seemed they could not get away soon enough. Emil remembered his mother often talking to him of the day when he should take a wife. She often told him to watch out and see that she was clean and good and industrious.

"A woman can throw more out of the kitchen door in a teaspoon than a man can bring in the front door on a shovel," she used to say. Then her eyes would grow tender as she let them dwell on the smooth features of her first-born with love and pride.

"Emil, never treat your wife badly," she had said. "A person can die inside for want of kind words, yes, and love."

She never said a word to him against his father, yet he knew that she never wanted him to develop the overbearing traits of character that his father possessed. In response, he never told her in so many words that he would not be like his father, yet he promised her again and again that he would be kind and loving and thoughtful.

Both knew what the other was talking about, yet no word was said about the husband and father.

Emil never knew until after he was married and established in a home of his own just how bleak his own boyhood had been. Pa would not allow any family dinners, no get-togethers. He quarreled early with his sons-in-law and wanted none of them. They did not celebrate Christmas nor did they ever go out on a picnic. It was always "Get to work, you," or "We have no time for foolishnesses."

ONE DAY a queer thing happened. Emil had been out in the field mending fence when he saw his father drive toward town. That was the signal for him to go to the house for one of his rare visits with ma. It was what she lived for. He had seen that his father was in a rage when he drove past on the road. His heavy brows were knit in an angry scowl. Emil wondered vaguely what had happened to enrage him, though he was not overly curious, for it was not an unusual occurrence.

Ma told Emil of the terrible quarrel pa had had with a peddler who had come to the door that morning selling tin pans, buckets and nails, pots and kettles, and the like. The peddler had a large two-horse wagon with a varied stock of things inside that met the needs of people who could not get to town easily. He had many bolts of calico, iron pots, bullets, skillets, strainers, tea, coffee, needles, pins, and crockery.

He took in exchange old rags, tallow, smoked meat, eggs, butter, and cheese. Some way, father found out he was a Jew. That set him off, or so it seemed. He began to bargain so loudly and to haggle so closely that mother said she was ashamed for him.

Finally the Jew became angry and was about to go away without selling a thing. He gathered up his wares and started out, his face aflame with indignation. Father toned down at that, for he needed some of the things and did not want the man to go away without exchanging some of the stuff they had to trade. But after the bargains had been settled on and the peddler had been paid, pa began maligning the man for being a Jew. Words of hate and venom rolled off his tongue like jumping toads. Mother said she had to get up and leave the room, it made her so sick. They were both shouting so loudly that it almost burst her eardrums, she said.

Finally the peddler had enough of pa's insulting talk. He got out his money and wanted to take back the pots and pans and cloth he had sold. He said he did not want any dealings with a man like that; but pa wouldn't let him have them. The Jew got up and slammed out the door, shouting that he would never return. He had gone as far as his wagon, but pa could not resist one parting shot.

"Well, at least, we do not keep your old Jew Sabbath," he shouted. "We keep the sabbath of the New Testament, the one that Jesus started."

Mother had to laugh a little at that, for everyone knew that Hans Huener never honored any day if it did not please his fancy to do so.

"Keep the sabbath that Jesus started!" the Jew turned and faced Hans and shouted at him in great anger. "I will give you everything I own in this wagon and in my shop at home and in all of my warehouses if you can prove to me that your Jesus changed the Sabbath. I am not foolish, and though I am a Jew, I know a thing or two. Saturday is still the Sabbath, whether you Christians keep it or not. I am not a Christian, and I do not keep the Sabbath as I ought to do, and as Moses taught us to do, but Jesus never changed it, and that is a fact out of a history book."

Hans had no answer to this. He simply stared openmouthed for a long moment, and the Jew glared back. They both looked angry enough to cut each other's throat. Mother said that for once pa had not a word to say. Then the Jew climbed into his wagon, whipped his horse, and drove hastily off down the road.

Hans, who had intended to go to the barn, changed his mind and came into the house. He laid his old farm hat on top of the kitchen food safe, went into the sitting room, and rummaged around in the clothespress till he found the old German family Bible that had lain back on the shelf

13

for years. He sat and read for at least an hour before he had to get up and go off to town.

"I cannot see for the life of me how he can read the good words of des Herr Jesu and go on doing as he does. He ought to see he is not living the life that Jesu wants him to live," mother told Emil.

I T WAS the queerest thing. When Hans came home from town, without a word he went in and got the Bible and began again to read. He seemed so doggedly determined that if will alone could do it, the words he was looking for would have been etched in fire. He searched the old Book for days on end, his temper getting shorter the more frustrated he became. Finally he put the Bible back into the press, and never to the knowledge of any of his family did he look into it again.

Then, to the amazement of everyone, Hans began to keep the seventh day Sabbath. Why he did so, no one could fathom. He did not do it from any desire to make his life better, for he was just as hateful and high-handed as before. He still guzzled his lager beer and smoked his long-stemmed pipe. The only change he made was that he did not work or trade on Saturday, and he kept the day —kept it hatefully, angrily, and vengefully. He forced it on his hired man and he forced it on mother. He would not even allow her to fill the lamps after the sun went down on Friday night. He made Emil and Ernest work that day, so there was no way of knowing just what he expected of his family.

There was a small country school a quarter of a mile down the road and the children got all their schooling there—when Hans did not keep them out to work. He had no use for education for his children, and he let it be known. They were not even encouraged to complete the elementary work the small school offered, much less try for higher stakes. Hans thought that if they could figure up acres and pecks and bushels, that was enough to serve their needs.

Emil, seeing how his father was blighting the lives of his whole family, vowed that when he married he would never let his children suffer as he had. Sometimes he became so frustrated that he felt tempted to run away and never let his father see his face again. But he was restrained by his mother, who ought not to have had a straw added to her heavy burden.

Emil's resentment knew no bounds when he was forced to quit school. He had become deeply interested, and the schoolmaster that year was very kind and had often favored him. The teacher had told Emil that he had a good mind, and that he ought to do something with it. He had bought an algebra book and a Latin book, and began to help the boy, so that he would be better pre-

In the fall, when his classmates went back to school, Emil was plowing in the field next to the road, and could not help seeing them pass by. He felt shackled with hateful chains that he had not the stamina to break.

pared for high school. When pa found the Latin book one night, Emil was forbidden to finish the school year. But he had had a glimpse of the golden world he had never even dreamed existed, the world of history and of the treasures of the past.

In the fall, when his classmates went back to school, Emil was plowing the field next to the road, and could not help seeing them pass by. He felt shackled to the farm with hateful chains, which he had not the stamina to break. He was plowing winter wheat one day when Gilbert Johanson went by. Now, he thought, Gil could study Latin. He had stopped at the fence and he told Emil that he was going to study chemistry, too, and algebra, although he had not been nearly as good at arithmetic as he. Emil's soul turned to wormwood within him. He chafed under his unjust restrictions.

ERNEST, HIS YOUNGEST brother, was a strange child. He was not like the others at all. He was ten years younger than Emil, and smart as mustard. It was strange, but mother had her way about him. He was not taken out of school as the others were, but was allowed to go on to high school. Emil never knew quite how ma managed, but she did.

Ernest was a funny fellow. He had one blue eye

and one brown eye. But mixed as his eyes were, he knew what he was doing, and he went to school in spite of pa's snarls and threats. He was the only one in the house who was not afraid of the old man. Ma told Emil in an awed whisper that Ernie got away with murder with pa.

"You know, Emil, that boy just goes away whistling, as unconcerned as if the wind was blowing, and lets pa shout at the door. He don't act scared at all. One day pa got the buggy whip, and he told Ernie he was going to give him a schooling, so he'd know once and for all who was the boss. But Ernie just said, 'Oh, Pa; put that up. Somebody is going to get hurt if you don't.' Do you know, pa put it up? I never was so surprised. But I was scared, too."

Emil reveled in Ernie's spunk, for of jealousy he had little. He went on and wrought as well as he could under the circumstances. He let his father shout and complain and order him about. He went stolidly along, did as pa said, as far as he was able, and did not give him the back talk that Ernest did when he was older. Emil was approaching thirty when Ernest came home from high school one afternoon with the astonishing announcement that he had decided to be a doctor.

It was spring, almost time for school to be out, and Ernie came in joyfully, even gleefully. His entrance always brought a breath of fresh air into the house. The shadows seemed to lift, and everything looked brighter.

He took off his cap first, and sailed it in a sweeping arc to the top peg on the old hall tree. Then he took off his coat, and hurled it through the air, where it too, obedient to his expert aim, hung right on a nail. Things always went Ernie's way—even coats and hats.

It was about four-thirty in the afternoon. Emil had just come in with an armload of kindling for the big woodbin that was next to the kitchen range. Old Hans was sitting on a splint-bottom chair by the south window. He had the shoe last between his knees. He was expertly half-soling a pair of old work shoes. Mother was kneading bread in a large tin dishpan.

Ernie sat down and laid a bag of peppermint sticks down on the table beside ma. She loved stick candy, and Ernie knew it. She put the brown bag into her apron pocket and flashed one of her rare smiles at the boy. It was a queer smile, hardly a smile at all. It was more of a twitch of pleasure, so brief that it darted into her features only to dart out again as hastily as it had appeared.

Emil, seeing it, had longed to keep it there. To his weary fancy, her smile held a bright beauty. She had been such a pretty girl, he remembered by the pictures she kept in the bottom drawer of the old secretary bookcase. Had she dreamed dreams as he did, and was she dead inside because her dreams had come to nothing— and worse than nothing?

$\mathcal{M}$A KEPT GLANCING at Ernest's animated face as she molded the puffy bread dough into biscuits and laid them out on the iron griddle to rise. Both boys knew she had fried half a skillet of onions to a delicate brown, then kneaded them into the springy dough. Her onion rolls were almost a legend with her family. Both boys eyed the pan of fluffy rising biscuits hungrily.

"Well, Mother," Ernest had cried, his voice ringing out with exultation, "today I've made the most momentous decision of my life."

"Have you?" ma asked softly. "And what might that be, my boy?"

"Well, Mother, I have decided what to do with my life. You know, I just couldn't decide before. I thought at first that I would go to college and learn to be a lawyer. Later, I thought I'd take up teaching. But today I found a magazine that made me decide."

"A magazine, Ernie?" questioned ma. "What kind of magazine was it that could get you so excited?"

Ernie reached over calmly, took an apple out of a dish, and chomped down a big bite before he replied.

"Good Health," he answered. "One of the girls had it. She made a report in the class about an article in it. She is going to be a nurse, or something, I guess, and her report made me curious. Well, I got to reading this magazine and I decided to be a doctor. There's a medical school in Battle Creek, Michigan. I read the advertisement, and when I saw some of the pictures I tell you it got me all worked up. I found out that was what I was wanting to be all my life—a doctor."

If Ernest had knocked over ma's dish cupboard, it would not have caused a bigger tumult.

"A doctor!" shouted old Hans, leaping to his feet and fairly choking with rage. "No son of mine will be a pill peddler. I tell ye that doctors are the worst passel of thieves in this United States. I won't have it, and so I tell you! You can jest stop that goin' to school and start plowin' tomorrow with Emil. You'll do it, yah, or I'll show your back how it feels to have this harness laid across it, like you've been needin' fer a long time."

Ernest merely leaned his chair back against the wall and faced his father calmly, not batting an eyelash.

"No, you won't do that, and neither will I quit school," he answered smoothly and unperturbed. He sat there and whistled under his breath in the blackest kind of silence, and tapped his pencil on the edge of ma's wooden kitchen table.

Ma had finished her buns and was cleaning her breadboard, and Emil, standing incoherent at the door and watching the little drama, noticed that her fingers trembled violently. Ernest must have noticed it too, for he reached right over and laid one strong boyish hand over her thin fingers. Her whole body suggested the frail, sapped-out sweetness of a pressed flower. Ernie smiled at her boyishly.

"Never you mind, Ma," he had said, though how he could do it so gaily Emil could only dully wonder. He marveled at his brother who by a pure miracle was old Hans's son.

"Don't get worked up, Ma; it doesn't worry me a bit. When I get to be a doctor I'll buy you the prettiest black taffeta dress in all of New York."

Ma's chin trembled pitifully as she looked at her boy. If he, by some miracle of alchemy, could have bought for her an hour of happiness it would have been like heaven to her poor starved heart.

As soon as he could, after Ernest's flip answer, Hans slammed out of the kitchen; and it was a good thing for all concerned, ma especially. She always relaxed visibly when he left the room.

She seemed to live for the moments of Ernest's wholesome exuberance, which was her chief happiness in life. No one could buy happiness for her, and she had to find it where she could.

Strange to say, in spite of pa's wild threats he said no more against Ernest's going. He seemed to realize he could not do a thing about it and must face the boy's independence as one faces facts that can't be changed.

WHEN SCHOOL was out and Ernest had received his diploma, he packed the small trunk that ma had brought over from Germany in the hold of the old ship, and left eagerly for Battle Creek. Pa would not even tell him good-by. He would not have had the money for his train fare if Emil and ma had not chipped in to give it to him. Ma had sold a few eggs and chickens at the door, and Emil had the small wages that pa had grudgingly doled out in fear that he might go somewhere else.

Ernest soon got settled, and the letters that came home were marvels to ma and Emil. Ma and the rest kept still about the letters, for pa had torn one up before ma had a chance at it. After that the postman handed them to Emil, or kept them at the post office till he came to get them. Ma seemed to live from letter to letter. Ernest's letters were alive with the news of the wonderful place where he had elected to spend several years of his life.

Emil was astonished when he learned that the college and sanitarium and medical school were all regulated around the seventh-day Sabbath. It was not very pleasant news, for pa's Sabbathkeeping was not popular with his family, or with the neighbors either. Emil was amazed at the attitude Ernest took toward that fact, for he and his brother had talked it over again and again and declared that the keeping of the seventh-day Sabbath was the craziest thing pa did, and that was saying a great deal.

Ernest had written, " 'Sure, they keep Saturday here, but not like pa does at all. These people here are really Christians, as far as I can see, and let me tell you, I look around a lot. Here at this big sanitarium they don't give medicine like that which most of the doctors do, and they treat disease mainly by water treatments and diet. They don't eat flesh meats, not even fish. And no teas or coffee, either. You never saw the like of it.

" 'People are here for treatment from everywhere, and let me tell you, there are moneyed people too. I saw an old man down on the lawn today from Germany talking to an elderly woman from London. This place is known all over the world.' "

Ma made a tut-tutting sound, she was so amazed at the news Ernest's letters always brought.

" 'I went and heard a lecture last week at the church about how this health work began,' " read Emil, continuing the letter. " 'From what I remember of it, they began it in a frame house right after the close of the Civil War. They began right away treating diseases in the natural way, by using right foods, sunshine, exercise, and water treatments. I tell you, it's great, and it works, too. I've seen people come here half dead from dosing with calomel and laudanum and nux vomica, and I've seen them raised right up by all these natural treatments till they hardly knew themselves.' "

"That calomel is awful," ma offered. "My poor sister Bess took too much once, and I tell you, it ruined her health for life. But go on, Emil, before pa comes in."

" 'People come from everywhere, Dr. Kellogg told us, and he said that even when they first opened the sanitarium the patients came so fast that the men could hardly get the equipment moved in. And the house was fixed up till it was really elegant in the eyes of the folks round about.

" 'They installed a great big windmill, he said, and a storage tank up high over the roof. If there is any breeze at all, it pumps water up the eighty feet into the big storage tank at the rate of a barrel every three to five minutes. That beats going to the pump for every drop of water, doesn't it, Ma? Folks around here never saw a thing like that. The water from the top tank flows down to a tank above the treatment rooms where they give baths to the sick folks. There are tanks that heat the water to any heat required. I call that pretty good for the days when only wealthy homes had a bathroom.

" 'From what I gathered, they did away with coffee, and tobacco, and tea to begin with. Then it was about a year later, I think, that they began to try the meatless diet; and that was a success from the very first.

" 'Someone has opened a little restaurant about a block away, hoping that the patients who can't abide the vegetarian diet will supplement with them. They handle all the stuff the san frowns on, but you'd be surprised—they don't get the business they had counted on.

" 'Ma, I am going to send you a can of Protose. It is a meatless meat food, made out of nuts and different stuff, and I really like it. It is made at a food factory here run by the san.

" 'I am putting on weight, and I never felt better in my life. I haven't eaten a bit of meat of any kind since I left home.' "

EMIL WONDERED, and ma was disturbed mightily, and told Emil she was afraid that Ernest's health would suffer if he did not have good strong meat to build muscles and bones. He ought to have food he was used to, she thought.

"Well, I reckon you don't need to worry about Ernest and his not eating meat," Emil told her. "Ernest has a head of his own, and he said he was feeling fine, the best he has ever felt."

"I know he said that, Emil," ma said, "but if he ain't getting the right food, he won't be well very long. It doesn't take long to break a young feller's health down."

"I don't know, Ma," Emil answered. "I guess cows are strong, and elephants—and they live on greens. I heard that Benjamin Franklin did not eat meat, and he was one of the wisest men of the early days of America. I guess it didn't hurt him."

"I never heard of that," ma said eagerly, not a little comforted at the assurance that her dear Ernest did not stand in danger of hurting his health.

"And I have heard of that place where he is too, Ma, and it is a big place. I read once that the Dr. Kellogg Ernie mentions is counted to be one of the wisest doctors in the world. I heard about their treatments with water and no drugs. I even heard pa talking about them one day, for it is a Saturday college, and you know how he dotes on keeping Saturday, since he had the quarrel with that Jew."

Mother smiled wanly. There was no real amusement in her smiles, as Emil could always remember. He did not recall ever seeing her really smile or even laugh.

"If only pa would do one thing from principle rather than from spite," she had said, "I believe he would find the happiness he has never known—and would let the rest of us find it too. But he never will. He is a slave to his own iron will. And he makes us slaves too. But not Ernest," she rejoiced fiercely. "Not Ernest."

After Ernest had been at the medical school about a year a letter came addressed to Emil himself. That was surprising, for mostly the letters were sent to ma, though Emil shared them with her.

He told Emil that he was going to be married, and he said that his wife-to-be was also taking the medical course. It was a great life, he wrote enthusiastically, and he never was so happy. He had never really lived till he broke loose from the lead strings and got away. He would not change place with a king.

" 'I was talking to one of the profs about you the other day, Emil,' " he had written. " 'He told me that they would help you to put yourself through, and help you to get a start, if you came. No use to pity pa. You will die of dry rot if you stay there—and pa can get help. He has the money to do it; he has been salting down money in the bank for many a year, and he can pay. I pity ma, and I pity him, too, in a way; but no one is so blind as a person who will not see. Don't let him wreck your life, Emil. You still have time to make something of yourself.' "

Emil was reading the letter aloud to his mother. He looked up and saw the tears streaming down her cheeks. His heart plunged in sympathy. Poor ma. What was life giving her? Not much else but hard work, harsh words, and few comforts. But what about himself? Pa was stealing his life too. It was wrong to steal a life. It's just like stealing money. Where was he headed anyway?

Emil stopped reading and sat looking out of the kitchen window. A picket fence, unpainted and weatherbeaten, surrounded ma's vegetable garden. He saw that one of the cows had broken out of the pasture and was getting at ma's cabbages. He'd have to——

But where was he headed? He never went to church from one year's end to the other. He had no social life. Other young folks managed to have fun at the singing schools and the spelling schools and strawberry-and-ice-cream sociables, but not he. He had never had a girl. It was just work, work, work, twelve to sixteen hours a day. And to what end? Maybe Ernest was right. Maybe he should clear out, and——

As if she read his thoughts, ma spoke out bravely.

"Ernest is right, Emil—go. You have a right to your life too. You need have no regrets, for you have been good and faithful for years, and you have not fought against pa as much as I have wished you would—not that I like quarrels, no, but you have a will, and judgment too, and it grieves me to see you crushed all the time. Father will get along. He has money put away—lots of it. He brings in a lot and spends very little."

IT WAS IN that year of 1899 that Emil told his father that he was going away to the college in Battle Creek. He tried to tell it casually so as not to arouse a storm. But pa was furious. He gave Emil one look that would have killed, if looks could, and slammed out of the house and went to the barn. What hurt most was that he would not even say good-by when he finally went. He had given pa years of faithful service—it didn't seem fair.

Ma told him not to mind. She told him that he was doing what was right.

"You must not let a thing stand between you and an education," she told Emil that last day. He was to see a day when he wished with all his heart that he had heeded her admonition. She gave him all the money she had, and he had some, so he managed to buy his railway ticket. He went to Battle Creek with a heart full of hope. He had less than three dollars in his pocket when he got there.

He moved into his room, and to his country-bred eyes it looked absolutely palatial. He gazed out the window at the busy street. Horses and rigs of all kinds seemed to be passing continually. The big sanitarium up the street was the center of a hive of buzzing activity. Cabs pulled by shining black horses, hacks, carriages grandly upholstered with puffy black wool and topped by a fringed top, spring wagons, bicycles weaving in and out, almost made him dizzy. It was seldom that three conveyances a day passed their farm at home on its quiet back road.

Emil had to start right in with college preparatory courses, for he had not attended high school as had Ernest; but he did not mind. He was not alone. There were many in the same boat. There were farm boys from the South and the West and the Middle West who were new converts to whom Battle Creek was a mecca. Here was a sanitarium and a food factory where work in abundance might be had, a college where first-class learning was dispensed, and a publishing house where the books that had appeared on their bookshelves had been printed. Emil got work in the sanitarium kitchen, washing such gigantic pots and pans as he did not even dream existed. In this place food, delectable yet strange beyond description, was prepared for the ailments of sick people from every corner of the earth.

The young man was at first astonished, for from the way he saw them going about things, he had never seen such cookery before in his life.

He sent one recipe home to ma, as he saw them prepare it, after a clean white snow had fallen. They called it "snow gems." It was so good that he wanted ma to share it.

"Beat together lightly, but thoroughly, two parts clean, freshly fallen snow, and one part best granular corn meal. Turn into hot gem irons, and bake quickly. The snow should not be packed in measuring, and the bread should be prepared before the snow melts."

You would not believe how good it was.

Instead of the pork chops and side meat and ham that sputtered in rivers of lard in his mother's black skillets, and the great dishes of greasy fried potatoes, meat roasts and sausages, head cheese and blood pudding, there was an entirely different approach to food.

Oil was used, not lard. Cream was used more often than butter. The sanitarium bakery turned out beautiful brown loaves of whole-wheat and graham bread, and whole-wheat and graham crackers. Milk came in twice a day from the sanitarium cattle, and cottage cheese, fresh-made, hung draining above the sinks in cheesecloth bags. The dry curds were freshly added to sweet clotted cream just before it was served.

Both Irish and sweet potatoes were baked and served with sweet cream. The nut foods, Protose and Nuttolene, were prepared deliciously in dozens of ways. They were crumbled and blended with hard-cooked eggs—the chickens were owned by the place—mixed with celery, braised onions, and lemon juice, and baked with peeled potatoes under a bubbling brown gravy. Often they were mixed with tomato, herbs, and onions. Such dishes were better than one would imagine. It was passing strange, but Emil's bilious spells stopped—the spells of nausea that he had had ever since he was a child. He did not have a single one as long as he was on the diet there at the Battle Creek Sanitarium.

In spite of the fact that Emil was an older student, he found great delight in his lessons, and he discovered to his joy that he was not the "dumb ox" that he had feared he would be. Ernest's self-assuredness had made Emil fear that he was not as bright as his shining younger brother.

But his teachers liked him, and he did wonderfully well. He got good grades in all his lessons, except music. That seemed hard at first, but after a while he caught on to what the teachers were talking about.

PROFESSOR G. H. BELL, who had been legendary in the early days of the college, still wielded his mighty influence in the grammar books that were textbooks in the English classes. Emil devoured English grammar and rhetoric eagerly. He got his best grades in these classes, much to his gratification. Once he wrote a theme on "Ambition," and the teacher read it aloud to the class. It was one of the happiest days of his life. He copied it and sent a copy home to ma, but he did not realize how glad it made her.

But one of the brightest days he ever had was the time when the teacher had to be absent and he asked Emil to conduct the class. He wore his best coat that day, and he washed and ironed his best shirt by lamplight the night before. Then he stood in front of that big class and asked questions and answered them, as he had heard his teacher do many a time. It awakened an ambition in his heart to

3 33

make something of his life. He was to remember this hour of triumph many times in the years that followed, and to grieve and to wish with all his heart that he had heeded that early impulse. He did heed it, after a fashion, and he had the backing of his younger brother, who urged him on and on and on.

Ernest was married to his Carrie the year he graduated, and they set up practice nearby; of this, Emil was glad. He needed their encouragement. He had many lonely hours, for he did not know how to mingle with the others, and was like a child who is turned loose among a lot of rollicking children, but who has never learned to play. He would go and spend long evenings with Ernest and Carrie.

"Take medicine, Emil," Ernest said one day. "I tell you what. You take up medicine and we will set up our offices together. I have decided to take some post work in surgery at Ann Arbor, and between us, we can—well, it will be an ideal setup."

"I'm in my thirties," Emil said. "Don't you think I'm too—well, too old?"

"Fiddlesticks," Ernest said airily. "Just old enough to begin to have horse sense."

"Yes, and Emil," Carolyn put in mischievously, "you'd better begin to look around for a wife; and be sure she is a nurse. She would fit into our setup like a dream. She could work for us and help you get through."

Emil protested at that. He did not want his wife working and digging and delving that way for him.

"Nonsense," laughed Ernest. Better have a little foresight than so much hindsight. Carolyn had helped him so much that he did not see how he could have made it without her. "You see, she graduated a year before I did, and let me tell you, she helped me to swim! Without her help I'd have sunk for sure."

Even though it was a joke, or maybe it was half in earnest, Emil the bashful began to take notice of the girls in crisp uniforms, with tiny starched and fluted caps that looked like paper muffin cups perched on grand puffy pompadours. Some of them still in training wore blue-and-white dresses covered with snowy aprons, so smoothly ironed that they looked as though they had been cut from sheets of stiff white bond paper.

They all looked lovely, and were a contrast to the girls he met when he had to go to town, or those whom he saw in the stores. In the halls, on the lawn, on the sidewalks, these consecrated young ladies were flitting like butterflies. They were walking with patients, sitting with them, wheeling chairs, or running about in their endless work of ministry. Emil could concur with Ernest that a nurse was a very desirable kind of person with whom to link up his lonely life, especially if he decided to be a doctor. If he decided on that, then there could be no other person more fitted as a companion.

ONE DAY in chapel Dr. Kellogg had the hour. He was a bundle of ambition and activity. He always wore white, winter and summer. One wondered, looking at him, how his busy mind must have worked. Emil chuckled a little, looking at him, and thought of the really great things he had done and the surgical instruments he had invented. Yet he was not above going into the kitchen and spending hours over some invention in the line of a meat substitute, or suggesting something to make the diet more palatable for those who were taking the step into vegetarianism. It was not enough for the little man that it be good for his patients, but it must taste good and be a substitute worthy of the name. Someone told Emil that the doctor had made a kind of butter out of peanuts, which he called peanut butter. It really tasted good if you spread it on bread and cut up a sweet onion on top. It filled you up. Emil told Ernest he would predict that it would take hold like wildfire, for every boy in the land would be crazy about it if he got a taste of it.

On this occasion, in the college chapel the doctor, with his inimitable zest and fire, was telling how the health message could pave the way for real evangelism in the great cities of the United States. He told the students that the best way they could serve the Lord was to learn how to live in good health and to learn how to teach people to avoid disease. He told how the nurses in the sanitarium often went beyond the call of duty in relieving pain and suffering and explained that it was the second-mile experience that really counted in the long run.

That he was proud of his sanitarium full of efficient nurses, whose integrity was almost proverbial, was all too evident. To one of the nurse's evident discomfiture he named her as a shining example of what an ideal nurse should be. It was Jeanie Marlow, and Emil stole a look at her, for she sat right across the aisle from his chapel seat. Her cheeks were as red as the roses that blew in the dooryard at home. All the time the doctor was talking she looked down at her crisp apron and did not look up once. This pleased Emil, her being so modest and so shy, even when the doctor was telling of how her quick work in an hour of emergency was the means of saving a patient's life. The patient was so grateful that he inquired into the religion of this young woman who had saved his life.

The week before, when Sophie Southwertz was mentioned in connection with some experience she had had in one of the poor homes in the city, Emil had noticed that she had held her head up proudly, as much as to say, "That is *I*; they are talking about *me*." Sophie was like that anyway, and it was well known that she liked the fanfare and the limelight whenever she could capture it. But not Jeanie, Emil thought. Not Jeanie. Emil feasted his eyes on her dainty features, and the soft color came

37

and went on her sweet lovely face. Jeanie, Jeanie, thought the young man, you are the one I have been looking for all my life. He had never so much as considered going with a girl. He was so shy and backward, and at home he had felt himself too ignorant for the kind of girl he would like. At home he knew none of the more educated girls; and the extremely poor and ignorant ones who lived in the village, he was not interested in. He had no idea how to go about winning this queen among women. At first he was in a fever lest she was already promised, for he could not imagine that a girl as attractive as she would not be spoken for. Then, by discreet inquiry, he learned that though several had admired her, she had given her heart to none of them. Then he worried that she would give him the cold shoulder as she had the rest. And looking at himself in the mirror, he groaned aloud. How could any-one so sweet and dainty as she have a thing to do with a big rough country yokel like him?

Emil would have stoutly denied it, but he was really a very personable man. Still apple-cheeked, and stockily built, there was a wholesomeness and an honesty about him that was winning. His blond hair lay in waves even though he combed it securely and roached it back, as was the fashion in that day. His eyes were as blue as the sea he had crossed as a young lad from Germany.

It was Brother Ernest who came to the rescue and helped him to get acquainted with her. Carolyn knew her well; so it was natural for Emil to stroll in on an evening when Jeanie had been invited to take dinner with the family. The matter of getting acquainted didn't prove to be much of a hurdle after all. They had a merry time talking and chatting, for it seemed they all "spoke the same language," the language of the healing art, and of the medical profession. When Jeanie learned that Emil had his eyes on the medical course, she looked at him with new interest, for his brother Ernest was already gaining himself a reputation for his skill in diagnosis.

Even in those days, in nursing schools and colleges marriages were not permitted during the school year, and even courtship was frowned upon, for it was thought that it would hinder the student from doing his best in his studies; and that was right. Any courtship was frowned upon at any time, especially if it was conspicuous. Emil wanted to maintain his high marks and avoid talk as much as he could, yet he did not want anyone to get ahead of him in the matter of winning Jeanie. That really created a problem, and how to solve it he did not know. But Ernest stepped in again and helped out.

Ernest or Carrie would let him know when Jeanie was calling on them, and Emil found it wondrously convenient to drop anything he might be doing and pay his brother a visit. He did not let his lessons suffer, for he was determined to get the requisite courses done in preparation for the premedic work to which he was looking forward. He had been long enough around Battle Creek for the medical work to get into his blood, and now here was the nurse, whom Emil had begun to think liked him —at least a little. Ernest had told him once that her face lit up like a Christmas tree when she heard his step on the stairs, but Emil could hardly believe it—he must have been mistaken.

Of course, Jeanie never said a thing to encourage him, for nice girls did not do those things in those days. Even so, she did not repulse him, and in spite of himself, he felt his courage rising, though he could not for the life of him understand what she could see in him. He was years behind her educationally, socially, and professionally. He thought bitterly of how his father with his hard-headed ideas about life had nearly wrecked his life. Pa's contempt of education, and of books and the book way of doing things, had nearly dried the very sap out of his youth. Emil could see that there were better ways, and he had borrowed magazines and farm books. But just let him broach some new idea and his father would fairly hoot him out of the house. Well, if he had not taken his foot in his hand, as the old saying goes, he would have lived and died a stick-in-the-mud. It was a pity he had not "lit out" and left long before he did.

WO YEARS FLED by on the wings of time and busy work. Emil was through with his preparation and was at last ready to embark on his lifework. He and Jeanie had decided that they would marry, and she would nurse and help him achieve his life ambition.

They walked out one Sunday to look for houses or rooms to set up housekeeping. They ranged all the streets around the sanitarium and the college, searching for just the right place. Not a large house, for it would mean too much work, and the next four years would be hard at best. Yet they did not want any cramped little place where you had to step out into the hall to change your mind.

Finally they both were satisfied with a small apartment they found in a house built on a hill, so that the basement apartment was actually on the first floor and opened on the small lawn that bordered on the back street, while the owners had an opening on the front street. The place gave them a sort of privacy that none of the others had, and they both liked it. The kitchen was a large neat room with a wood stove, a small sink, and a built-in corner cupboard. The wallpaper was clean, with a pattern of Dutch windmills.

"I could set the kitchen table here, Emil," Jeanie had said excitedly. "And we could eat here for everyday, and use the dining room for Sabbaths and when we have special company. And I could have red geraniums on that side window sill. Oh, Emil, it will be fun keeping house for you, dear!"

"And it will be like heaven to have you—to keep house for me, and to have you with me for always, my sweetheart," he had answered, his heart full of love for her.

The apartment had a bedroom that had only one small window, which Emil deplored, for he liked air and plenty of it when he slept; but Jeanie pointed out that it was on the shady side of the house and would not get the hot sun in the summertime. Besides, hadn't he noticed that the nights were often quite comfortable even though the days were hot? And the pretty sitting room, with three wide windows opening onto the lawn, was prettier than any they had looked at, and Emil was convinced.

But they did not rent the apartment. When Emil got back to his room that night, there lying on the hall table was an unlooked-for letter from pa, of all things. It was the first he had ever received from him, and Emil was touched at the tone of it, for the proud man had gotten off his high horse more than Emil had ever seen him do before. Ma had written regularly and had kept them in touch with the life as they had known it before they left for Battle Creek.

Emil hardly knew his father's handwriting, he had seen it so seldom. He had seen it a few times on documents, a labored, shaded old-world script, precise, and as neat as copper plate. As soon as he read the letter he was so filled with astonishment that he hurried over to Ernest's to share it with him.

"I do not believe that I will live so very long," the letter stated boldly. "You know the hired man, Fritz, who has been with me so long? Well, he has married and has gone to farm for his wife's father, and I can't blame him. A man likes to be on his own land. Adolph wants to go and take a course to be a horse doctor, but where he got such an idea I cannot say. Certainly not from me." Emil and Ernest could whole-heartedly concur in this. "Now, this leaves ma and me on the acreage, and it is more than I can do at my age. Now, Emil, here is my proposition: Ma and I will go and live in the tenant house on the west forty. I will farm that, and you can do as you please with this 160 acres that go with this big house.

"I seem to remember that you were always having ideas of doing things some new way—ideas that I did not like at the time—and I have often thought since that I was a fool to discourage you. You might never have got the idea to leave here if I had let you be, but a man gets to thinking sometimes he will always be around to see that things go the old way—and I like the old ways best. But I was thinking the other day of how my own father used to be angry, how he would growl because his own father, my grandsire would cling to ways that were old, while my father leaned toward the new. I guess we get so we like the ways we have struggled to work out, and we forget there might be new things coming up in every generation."

T HERE WAS VERY little more to the letter except to tell Emil that if he would leave off going to school and come on home, pa would go to town with him and make the place over to him. The only thing Emil had to promise was that he would take care of the place and of the old folks as long as they lived. And in return he would get one of the best farms in the whole country.

Emil thought for days about the proposition. The farm was, indeed, a wondrous place, fairly hewn out of the wilderness. There was a fine river, many springs cold as ice, and meadowlands, woods, and soil on the fields black as coal and as rich as the best. A stream clear and never-failing ran right through the meadow, so that watering the stock was never a problem.

Emil had had dreams of a vast stock farm with milk sheds and perhaps even a bottling plant, with the cream separators that go with it. When he had ventured the idea to pa, he had hooted at it, and Emil had reluctantly given it up. There was one spot, back about a hundred yards from the barn, where a natural spring bubbled out of the

44

side of the hill, and Emil had often stood and watched it leaping down the hill and becoming a merry little brook. He had longed to harness it and make it into the perfect cooling plant for the dairy of his dreams. There were dollars in this place, and he could get them out if pa would only give him a little say-so. But he never had. Now things were different. Why, pa was actually making a gift to him of the farm and the house, and Emil well knew the value of the gift. He knew every acre, every spring, woodland, and field in the whole place.

Then he began to weigh what it would mean if he took the offer. He tried to be honest with himself, and consider every factor involved. At the best it would take him five years to complete his medical course, and he was far from young. It would take him at least five more to establish a practice and to buy office equipment, furniture, and the other things he would like to have. It would take ten long years, and Jeanie would probably have to nurse the whole time to help him to get started. He talked it over with Ernest and Carrie for hours at a time. They were both dead set against it, and they hooted at the idea of its taking so long to launch a medical career.

"You will see, Emil—you will find yourself sitting pretty almost before the ink is dry on your sheepskin. I did; I stepped right in on a good practice when old Doc Ferguson died. You can do that too. We will keep our eyes open for a place——"

But Emil was determined to look at the thing fairly and weigh it from every angle. Ernest lost his patience.

"Now, listen, Emil," he said, pulling his chair up and grabbing his brother by the lapel of his coat. "You must know that father has not grown a set of wings nor developed a halo. He is still pa. I would wager that if you could talk to ma you would get a true picture of things. Wait till you get a chance to hear from ma. I don't trust pa, and never did for that matter. His soft words don't butter any parsnips as far as I am concerned."

Emil did not answer right back, even though pa had asked for an immediate answer. But he could not get away from the fact that he was already in his thirties; he was sure he could start right out making money if he went to the old home place and took up pa's proposition. He had dreamed so much in those days of frustration and futility that he persuaded himself he would know right where to begin, and that in a matter of a few weeks he could step into comparative security.

He talked it over with Jeanie freely, for she was not prejudiced, as in her inexperience she had judged Ernest to be. Of course, she did not know in the least what was involved, as Ernest did know, and as Emil should have known. He elaborated at length on the possibilities of the place and what could be done if he had the free hand with it, as pa had indicated. Naturally, it looked good to her, especially when Emil told her that if she did not want to lose out on her profession, she could nurse any time she wanted to get some extras for herself, though he did not think it would be at all necessary.

As THINGS TURNED out, the week before he was to have enrolled in the medical course he was on the train, speeding for the homestead farm, for which he had bartered the biggest dream of his life. All he could think of was the fact that it would be his, all his, and he could hardly sleep at night for thinking of it.

They had decided that he was to go on ahead and get things ready, and Jeanie was to stay and get things together for the wedding they had agreed would take place as soon as things could be arranged. He needed to get the legal matters settled, and help ma and pa move to the other house.

"I will let you know what I am doing, and as soon as I see how much I must do, I'll have some idea of how long it will be," Emil told Jeanie in the letter he wrote on the train.

"I want to drill a well up near the house. Pa wouldn't do it, so poor ma had to have her water carried nearly all her married life, and many times she had to carry it herself. I want things easier for you. I want the house more convenient—I don't want my wife to have it as ma did while she was raising us children. And I am going to fix things in the house where they are moving, so ma can have it easy. I don't want ma to lose a thing by moving away from this house.

"You just ask ma when you get here, Jeanie; she will tell you that I always tried to help her and make her life as easy as I could, ever since I was a boy."

Even though everything looked promising, and Emil did make a success of his venture from the very beginning, he was to regret all his life the decision he had made. "If only I had not listened—if only I had gone on with medicine," he had said afterward again and again, until he was convinced in his heart that the train ride he took that cold fall day was the turning point in his life.

Pa did all that he promised, and ma was glad to see him, but Emil sensed the very first day that she did not think he should have come. He helped them move and he fixed ma's kitchen first thing with a pitcher pump and a sink, the first one she had ever had in her life. He enclosed the back porch and painted all the woodwork, and she hardly would have known her old furniture when he was through with it. She was as pleased as a child.

With that done, Emil turned his attention to the big sprawling house in which he had grown up. It was well built, for Hans did his work strongly, though without artistry of any kind. It was all incredibly ugly, and Emil could see it now for he seemed to see it with Jeanie's eyes.

He would completely renovate the house and make it a bit presentable and more modern, to say the least. When not busy with the winter chore work, he was constantly at work with plans and hammer and tools, working like the wind far into the night. It was wonderful how quickly he made vast changes, much to old Hans's disgust. To Emil's relief, the old man said nothing, though his black glances of disapproval spoke volumes. But the old folks moved away without a word, for the papers were signed now and the place belonged to Emil. The deed was in the strongbox up under Emil's bed, and he had signed, too, that as long as he lived the old folks would be cared for in sickness and health. If either one of them got sick, Emil told himself, he was marrying a nurse that even Dr. Kellogg had said was one of the best.

Ma had her hens and pa had the best Jersey cow and a pig. Emil had sold the rest. It was as Hans told Emil—they could make out very well on what he could make on the forty. With ma's butter and cheese and the eggs, they could do the trading in town and get all the things they would need. And the garden and the field would take care of the rest.

Emil got the dairy going first of all. He worked early and late on the natural cooler that he had dreamed of as a boy, and winter had scarcely passed before he had the spring piped and harnessed and the stone dairy house well begun. The field-stone building was built over a series of tanks from which the spring flowed into a brook that went down into the sheep pasture. In these shallow tanks, built and floored with flagstones, he could visualize the crocks of butter, cheese, and cream, and the rich milk for which he was sure to have a ready market. Here the butter would be kept sweet even in the hottest days.

He worked like a machine from early morning till the moon rode high at night. By spring he had to have two hired men to take care of the growing trade of the dairy. Pa came over and for once he was approving. Once he told Emil that he wished he had let him do it when he had wanted to when he was at home. That grudging admission of his father did Emil a world of good. Just to see approval on his father's hard-bitten old face was something to really rejoice about. A cart came every day and picked up the produce. Emil had ma come over, and she was put to work supervising, until she was making money of her own. She sang in a quavering old voice as she directed the work of the farm girl, who seemed to be churning the old barrel churn from sunup to sundown. Things were looking up, and Emil's letters to Jeanie fairly dripped enthusiasm.

Finally he got the house done. He went into debt for the furniture, though he had not really meant to do so. It all came from a desire to please Jeanie and he decided to have their wedding in their own home, right by their own fireside.

"It seems to me it will be an omen of a good beginning, Emil," Jeanie had written in one of her letters, "to start out in our own home and with our own things like that."

Emil had agreed enthusiastically, and had thought it a good idea until he began to look critically at the old furniture that ma had generously left in the house. The place where they had moved was small, so they had taken only their bedroom suite, the kitchen things, and the things from the back sitting room.

But the more Emil looked at the ugly, worn old furniture, which had been secondhand when Hans had undertaken to furnish the house, the more his heart misgave him. The dining table was covered with white rings where hot dishes had been placed on it through the many years. The chairs had been reseated at various times, and with different kinds of material. The bedrooms were equipped with ancient beds with sagging springs and stained, sodden mattresses, and the rugs were so old and threadbare that they had lost all claim to color or pattern. Even the window shades, cracked old silesia ones, were torn and patched again and again. Hans had been able to get better for ma, but he never would. Seeing the place through Jeanie's eyes, Emil felt a new pang of sympathy for poor ma, who had never had a thing to do with or to delight in; and he realized there had been no need for the misery that had been her lot. He would not treat his wife that way!

He had to get new kitchen and bedroom furniture, and there was no doubt about it. So he went into town to the local furniture store and began pricing things. He had thought to get a parlor suite upholstered in flowered Brussels and a new carpet for the parlor, as well as a bedroom suite, for ma and pa had taken theirs and the downstairs bedroom did not have a thing in it but an old broken-down stuffed chair. He simply had to get a new stove for the kitchen and a kitchen table and chairs.

The furniture salesman must have had a good sales line and must have believed in Emil, for he sold the young man far more than he had intended to buy. Every time he saw a shiny item of furniture he thought of how pleased Jeanie would be if she had that and how horrible the old scratched and dilapidated stuff was that now filled the house. He finally threw caution to the winds and bought everything new. He worried himself almost sick all the way home, but kept telling himself that he was going to pay it off as fast as he could lay his hands on the money. He hardly slept a wink that night, for the influence of years of penury and near stinginess made him doubly conscious of what he had done.

By morning his spirits had risen, and when the men came that day to paint and to hang new wallpaper all over the house, he got back the courage he needed. He painted the splintery old floors upstairs a nice battleship gray and laid carpet on the stairs. He fixed up Otto the hired man's house with ma's old furniture, all of which he repaired and either varnished or painted, till he could hardly credit his own eyes.

Finally the new carpets were laid in the parlor, sitting room, and dining room, and a bright checked linoleum was laid in the kitchen. The walls gleamed with new paper. The kitchen had patterns of cornfields, with ripe pumpkins and great sheaves of grain. With the clean white woodwork, the shining stove, and the new table, it did not seem like the same place.

The dining room was really very grand, for the china closet was filled with a fine new set of dishes that the store gave to Emil because he had bought his whole bill of goods from them. The sideboard and the pretty square table were of shining golden oak. The most stylish of all his purchases was a walnut bedroom suite with a marble-topped bureau and a fine-looking mirror built and rosetted right onto the back of it. Emil was intrigued with the smaller dresser—built to look as if the great towering one had had a child. The furniture man had called it a commode. It was similar to the furniture he had seen so much in the big Battle Creek Sanitarium rooms, and held to be needed for making one's toilet in those days when few folks had bathrooms. He bought a new washbowl and pitcher, and other accessories that went with it, and he was proud of his choice, for they were a soft blue with three fat roses painted on the side. Poor ma came and helped him to put the place in apple-pie order, and she walked from room to room with Emil, hardly able to believe that this was the place where so many sad and unhappy years had been spent.

The bleak back porch, which had been the prey of the harsh north wind, Emil had enclosed, using sash and window glass from an old house on the place that pa had torn down years before. The timber and the windows had been stored in the tool room of the barn to be used if and when needed. Emil set up an old laundry stove out there and told himself he would get a small pipe oven so Jeanie could use this as a summer kitchen, so as to keep the rest of the house cool in the hot summertime. He set the old food safe out there that ma had given to him, and he painted it inside and out, making the old punched tin doors gleam and shine like new. There was a new glass-doored dish cupboard in the kitchen, set near the big wrought-iron range with its beautiful blue-speckled granite reservoir for heating water for dishes and the like. It was going to be handy for Jeanie to have water nice and hot right at her hand.

Now he was glad he had decided to start new, with new things. Jeanie was going to be a queen for sure, in a home they could be proud of from the very beginning.

She was to arrive on New Year's Eve, 1902. Emil's aunt, who lived in town, was to meet her, and they made it up that Emil was not to see her until the ceremony. His older sister, his aunt, and his mother prepared a feast to grace the wedding. Ma worked so proudly and importantly in the renovated kitchen, with the new dishes and the new pots and kettles. Emil sensed that it was a high day in the long succession of pleasure-empty days of her poor life.

THERE WAS a kind of surprise about the wedding. Two of Emil's old friends, neighbors, whom he had known all his life, came and asked that it be a triple wedding, for all the neighborhood was agog with curiosity about how Emil had fixed up the old house, and everyone wanted to be included, someway. The two young farmers were very decent about their request—since they were planning to be married soon anyway, it would be nice if it could all be done at once, and it would be an event that the folks would talk about for many a day, that is, if Emil's young woman did not object to their "horning in."

Emil wrote Jeanie right away, and she was delighted with the novelty of the thing and told Emil to go right ahead and plan it with his friends. It would be something for Jeanie to brag about among the girls—a triple wedding right by her own fireside. It meant three times as many wedding presents as they would have gotten.

Emil had a new suit for the occasion. He had scarcely donned it before he heard the sleighs coming with the other grooms. The brides were already there, spirited in by ma and the girls to the pretty upstairs bedroom. The Seventh-day Adventist minister from a nearby town was to perform the triple ceremony, and he was waiting by the fireplace, wearing his fine frock coat with the shining black satin revers, and holding his Bible in his hand. As the three young bridegrooms lined up on one side of the fireplace, Emil could see through his nice house, and with pride noted how spotless and lovely it was. The three watched the stairs to see when the girls would appear. The parlor was full of people. Every new chair and footstool was occupied, and the new sofa was crammed to capacity. The small fry, self-conscious in their best clothes, sat in awed silence here and there on the shiny new floors that bordered the rich carpets.

Jeanie wore a dark maroon dress that matched the red carnations in her dark hair. What the other two brides wore, Emil never noticed, for Jeanie filled his eyes and his heart. He was in such a daze that he wondered afterward whether he had made the proper nuptial responses. He must have, for the knot was tied—a treble knot it was. The minister had said, "William, do you take Jerusha?" "Carl, do you take Kathleen?" and "Emil, do you take Jeanie?"

Suddenly they were all around the heaped-up tables.

There were more kinds of cake than Emil had thought possible—marble cakes, coconut, pound, chocolate, applesauce, fig dream, Lord Baltimore. It seemed that every one of the neighbor women present had done her best on her favorite recipe.

But cakes were not all that was on the table for the delectation of the big crowd. The children, hungry and eager, had been herded to the kitchen and put under the care of Joanna, the wife of the hired man. The rest marched around and filled plates with the multitudes of goodies that were heaped upon the big table. Great platters of sliced homemade bread were flanked by pats of butter only that day churned fresh and sweet. The evening was full of merriment, and ma and her helpers had things cleared up almost before anyone realized it. All too soon everyone was bundling up to go home. The snow was shiny as crystal, and the sleigh runners creaked as the sleighs slid smoothly up to the door and received load after load of happy guests. At ten-thirty all the good nights had been said, and Emil and Jeanie were alone in their new home.

There was no wedding journey. They had both decided that. When they had prospered sufficiently, they would take a belated honeymoon to Germany, Emil had told her.

That evening, while they had been playing games and feasting, the thermometer had dropped to twenty-five degrees below zero, but the kitchen stove, the parlor heater, and the dining room fireplace had kept things fairly warm. There was a small airtight heater in the bedroom upstairs. After all the folks were gone, Emil had time to take Jeanie all over the house and show her their new domain and the things he had gotten for her. Her pleasure in his choice more than repaid him. She praised the bedroom furniture, the parlor suite, and the dining room furniture. She told him that she could have done no better if she had chosen them herself. His heart glowed as he watched her animated face, realizing that she was his and he need not tell her good-by any more.

They opened some of their wedding presents that overflowed the sideboard and the whole of the dining table, so eager were they. As it turned out, they had six bread plates, three cake pedestals, four wooden mixing bowls, and a dozen sets of sugar and creamers, besides dozens of other things. They laughed gaily, and Emil was kept busy folding the papers and rolling up the ribbons and strings as Jeanie put her treasures on display.

Then Emil put a big log in the fireplace and filled up the heaters and set the drafts, so that the fires would hold for a good share of the night. Jeanie took a flatiron that had been heating on the back of the stove and wrapped it in a towel to put at their feet. Their bedroom was far from warm, though the fires had been going in the house all day.

EANIE TOLD EMIL the next morning that he had better go to the station to get the things she had brought from Battle Creek, for they had come on the same train she had taken. It took the biggest wagon on the place to hold it all. Emil was amazed.

There was an Edison Graphophone and many cylinder records. The horn was shaped and painted like a gigantic morning glory, and Jeanie was proud of her good taste in selecting such a beautiful stand table to set it on. It was of quarter-sawed oak, with grandly carved legs. Each leg ended in a brass claw holding tight to a glass ball. These served as gliders for the legs. There was a new Crown organ with fancy scrollwork and carvings and lattice work. At each side of the instrument, above the keys, was a fancy round shelf for use as a lampstand. Emil laughed when he saw that. "What else will they think of?" he asked. Emil was proud that Jeanie could play the organ, and he was glad she had brought her violin, for he knew she was an accomplished musician. But there was another thing besides the dishes, the linen, the silverware, bedding, and pots and pans and kettles that interested her husband very much. It was a device called a magic lantern. A strong pressure lantern was lit, some slides were put in, and wonder of wonders, there was a picture on the wall where Jeanie had had him hang a sheet.

"I thought it might be the means of missionary work," she had told him. And indeed, the neighbors, hungry for anything new, were eager to see the new marvel and came often to view the pictures.

Among her pictures were some of Egypt and the Pyramids, Jerusalem, Paris, London, scenes in dark Africa, Shanghai, and literally dozens of others. Ma never tired of looking at the pictures. Watching her small, pinched face in the half-light one night as he was showing slides, Emil was happy that his coming home had brought his mother so much pleasure. But when he mentioned something of the kind to her, he was surprised and disturbed at her answer.

"Oh, Emil, I wish you had not come——" she had said quickly. But then, seeing his face, so cast down and disappointed, she hastened to add, "Not that I do not like to see you here; it does my old heart a lot of good. But Emil, I am sure you are going to be sorry. You know how you hankered after an education, and how you used to dream, Emil. Besides, you're terribly in debt. I'm afraid —afraid."

"Oh, Ma, I'll be all right," he assured his mother. "And besides, a good farmer can do as much good as a doctor—or a nurse, or a teacher—if he really knows his stuff."

His words sounded brave and big, and he knew them to be true, after a fashion, but in his heart the question persisted. Was he really doing what the Lord wanted him to do? Then he worried about the debts he owed. The hundreds of dollars he had gone into the red for the lovely furniture preyed on his mind, and he redoubled his energies to pay them off. He worked early and late, like one possessed. He sold everything he could from the farm, the poultry, and the storehouses.

The dairy had been a success from the very first. It was a needed industry in the little village, and he signed up nearly everyone for cream, milk, cottage cheese, and butter. The hired man's oldest son drove the milk wagon in early every morning. So, little by little, Emil saw his debts decrease.

Jeanie, with rare discernment, soon learned of his burdens and gave him several hundred dollars she had saved at nursing. Though it humiliated him to take it, she put him at his ease.

"But sweetheart," she laughed, "this is a partnership. When we got married I aimed to do my share, and I am proud to do it, too. What worries you is my worry too, and I want you always to remember that. We must not keep our worries from each other. We will lose something if we do."

But behind it all was the ever-present thought in Emil's mind: Was God behind the move? Did God want him and Jeanie on that farm? Did He want Jeanie to bury her God-given talent of ministry to the sick in body and soul? Then the camel, who had gotten his head into the tent of their lives, proceeded to get all the way in. Their efforts to liquidate their debts got them into a veritable fervor for money-making. Even after their accounts were all paid, money-making became an obsession to both of them. They talked it, served it up at meals, and thought of it continually. And as time went on and they had been married almost two years, the place became a beehive of activity.

Jeanie became such an efficiency expert that she loved to fix lunches and take them to Emil and the hired hand in the far fields, so that they need not waste their time coming to the house. The hired hand might have felt like complaining, if it had not been for the delightful meals. She would bring towels and soap, so that it took them only a matter of minutes to wash in the cool river. When they returned, she would have the prettiest picnic lunch laid out you ever saw. It saved a lot of time coming and going, and money-wise Emil told Jeanie that she saved him several dollars a month in so doing.

Emil was proud of Jeanie's meticulous housekeeping and her economical ways. Everything she did was a delight to him. He hovered over her cakes, her breads, and her canned fruits and vegetables, sure that no woman ever was as clever and as thrifty as his lovely Jeanie.

"Jeanie even sweeps the yard," Emil proudly told

ma one day. Ma looked up from the sock she was darning and shook her head soberly.

"Yes, Emil, but she ain't nursing or takin' care of the sick, as God must've aimed for her to do. Emil, you've heard her tell how the Lord answered her prayers and led her to Battle Creek. Do you think God changed His mind in her case—or yours, either, for that matter?"

"Ma, you make me feel bad," Emil had said.

"I feel bad too, son, for I feel it in my bones that you ain't where God wants you."

Emil went on home, but he always felt uneasy when ma talked that way. Down in his heart he knew that he and Jeanie had not taken their problem to the Lord in prayer before they made their move. And everyone, without an exception, had advised him against the move, for he had a high record of scholarship and had been told he would be a wonderful doctor. Even Dr. Kellogg took time from his busy schedule to talk to Emil.

"God led you away from home—He led you definitely to come here, didn't He?" he had asked in his crisp, terse voice. "Seems like I remember your telling of it one night in a meeting. Now, the thing is, are you sure it is the Lord who called you away or is it the Lord who is calling you back?"

But in spite of Emil's apprehensions, he was prospering. At first, because there was no church near at hand, when the Sabbath came, he and Jeanie would go and

A gust of wind had blown the small fire over to the old lattice around the foundation of the old veranda, and in the semidrought they were having, it was as dry as tinder. The whole house was ablaze.

get ma and they would have Sabbath school and church service of a sort. Emil would read something, or Jeanie would. Ma's poor face fairly beamed. But as the work got more demanding, they shortened it and shortened it, until the past six months they had omitted it entirely.

Emil was constantly telling Jeanie to let up on her busy schedule, for they were looking for their first baby. She seemed well, however, and kept up the same schedule of work she had undertaken from the first.

ONE BRIGHT SUMMER day Jeanie had walked almost a mile with the large basket of lunch. The hired man and Emil were all washed up when they spotted her coming, and Emil went to meet her, while Adolph fetched a jug of fresh water from the spring. She spread out the red-checked cloth on the grass, and Emil told her she should not carry that heavy basket or walk so far.

Jeanie had laughed delightedly.

"Oh, Emil, I am as strong as an ox, and I never felt better in my life. I am a nurse, and I know how to save myself. I won't overdo—I promise you, dear."

But Emil was worried nonetheless.

The hired man, Adolph, took one huge bite of chocolate cake that she had brought for dessert, then suspending the business of chewing, he lifted his head and sniffed audibly.

"Seems like I smell smoke," he offered.

"I do too," Emil had said. "I wonder——" Then he gave a terrible cry. Off across the ridge of trees toward the house a great plume of smoke arose. It was either his barn or his house. It had to be.

He stood up and looked for one terrible minute. They all looked. Then Adolph and Emil started running.

"Take it easy. Don't run, Jeanie," he had yelled back. "We will run ahead. Now mind, don't you overdo."

Before they had rounded the little grove of trees Emil was sure it was the house. Just before Jeanie had come with the lunch, she had swept up a little pile of trash from the dooryard to burn as she had done dozens of times before. A few twigs, some dry grass, some papers and some leaves—her yard was as tidy as her pantry. As near as they could figure, a gust of wind had blown the small fire next to the old lattice around the foundation of the old veranda, and in the semidrought they were having, it was as dry as tinder. The whole house was ablaze.

Now the organ, the violin, the stereoscope, the cake stands, the sugar and creamers were all burning up. Even the magic lantern. And only recently was the grand furniture they had labored so hard for clear of debt. Great tongues of flame were licking it all up greedily.

66

Emil stood and wept as the floors fell in on the treasures that he and Jeanie had heaped together. They had no insurance. As good a businessman as Emil was, he had neglected that. Fires happened to other people, he had thought, but they would not happen to him.

Jeanie bore up amazingly well. She was a comfort to them all. They went to live with ma and pa for a few days until they could decide what to do. The neighbors came in the next week, and they had an old-fashioned raising, just like the grandfathers and the grandmothers remembered in the olden days. The great heap of logs, from trees that Emil had felled the year before to clear a field, was made into a log house. It was Jeanie who suggested it. The idea had come to her like an inspiration. Why go into debt to build a house, she had asked. Why not make out some way until they could save up the cash to build the kind of house they wanted?

Once the idea got out, it rolled up like a snowball. The neighbors for miles around rallied to the novelty of the thing. They met at ma's house and decided to make it a real old-fashioned outing and a housewarming shower. Early in the morning of the house-raising day, the teams and the wagons began to arrive. One farm family brought a table and a few chairs. Ill assorted as they were, they were more than welcome. Carpetbags by the bushel were offered. One family brought a bureau and another brought a wood stove. By the side of the spool bed one family hauled down out of their attic was a cradle that Granny Johnson had bragged about so much. She told everyone that her own great-grandpappy was rocked in it when our country "fit agin England." A trundle bed was there, to shove under the spool bed. Jeanie was delighted. She walked about, exclaiming with delight over everything. The women set dinner on trestles out on the lawn, while the men notched and raised the logs. By nightfall the shell was up, and it was only a week or so till Jeanie had moved in. It was a big house with a lean-to kitchen and a partition between the front room and the bedroom. A huge fireplace of field stone dominated one end of the room. Emil ceiled and plastered the house, and it was exceedingly pretty when Jeanie put her deft touches everywhere. She began to braid rugs right away, and was at it whenever she was not busy with her other work. The trunk where she had stored the new baby's things, strange to say, was not burned. When the floors had fallen, it fell clear of the fire, so Jeanie was saved the chore of remaking clothes for the expected little one.

ONE DAY JEANIE was sitting and talking to Emil as they were eating breakfast. The log house was as neat as wax. Somehow the torn and wounded soul of the young man was healing. The ruffled curtains, white as the driven snow, the bright geraniums, the braided rugs, and the scrubbed table—it all had a beauty that Emil felt in his very soul.

"You know, Emil, I have the queerest feeling about our baby to be born. I would like to dedicate him to be a minister. Yes, Emil, before he is born, I would like to give him to the Lord."

Emil laughed.

"Him?" he asked. "How are you so sure it will be a 'him,' my dear? It might be a 'her,' and then all your dedication will come to nothing."

"Don't laugh, Emil," Jeanie said earnestly. "Since the fire I have felt the way your mother has felt. I have felt that we should not have come here, and that you should have gone ahead with medicine as you had wanted to do. I have thought again and again of what we talked about one day when we heard of that man going to Africa all by himself with his violin."

"Oh, you mean the missionary who died within three months of the time that he got there? Of malaria, I believe."

"Yes, someway, I've thought we ought to have volunteered to go and take up where he left off. I read last week where a missionary named Branch has taken up that unfinished work. Emil—it might have been us."

"Yes, dear," Emil said slowly. "But it is too late. We

have too many commitments now, and too much responsibility. I don't see any way to get out of my promise to pa. We will just have to dig in and make the best of it."

The day was cloudy and overcast, and every now and then it poured. It was the kind of day that got on your nerves, Jeanie told Emil, when he came in and got the milk buckets. After supper he had to go on horseback in a driving rain to get the doctor, but even so, before he got back young John was born. Jeanie was her own nurse, and things were in hand when Emil and the old general practitioner rushed into the log bedroom. It was not often he had such a patient. Emil drove over after ma, and little John was washed and dressed and put into the old, old cradle. He was a bonny child, fat and good. Even ma, whose worn hands had washed babies, soothed illnesses, and closed the eyes of death, said she had never seen a finer child. Of course, she could have been prejudiced—he was her first grandson.

Jeanie often looked down at her little minister-to-be. To her, he was the brightest, the most beautiful, and the most unusual baby ever born.

"John Huener," she whispered. "John Edward Huener. You will be Elder Huener someday, and I will be so proud to hear you preach. I will say, 'That is my son.' You will be gentle, kind, and good. I will help you so you will not make the mistakes we have made."

*T*HEN, WHILE THEY were so happy, there came a letter one day that cast a pall of sadness on them all. Ma came over, her poor hands trembling and tears spilling down her cheeks. All was not well with Ernest. They had had reports all along about his prosperity, his fine new offices, and the home he had built out near the lake. Carolyn had written ma, begging her to use her influence to get Emil to make a trip to Battle Creek to see if he could get Ernest straightened out.

He had quit going to church, Carolyn said. Lately he had taken to smoking cigars, and even drinking.

"He says it is necessary to do all that if we expect to get anywhere," she wrote. "We have all we need, but Emil, that does not make for happiness. If I thought that our house and possessions were estranging us, I would be glad if they would burn as yours did, for with all we have, we are not happy. I sit sometimes and think of the gay and understanding times we had together. Oh, Emil, if you and Jeanie had only stayed—now the worst is happening, for Ernest is dating his office nurse. It is not my imagination either. A lot of my friends have seen them together, and I do not know which way to turn. Won't you come? He might listen to you."

But Emil could not get away. Burdened with his expenses, he was doing the work of three men; one of the cows was sick, and pa had an attack of lumbago. His chores fell to Emil.

He and Jeanie answered Carolyn's letter as well as they could, and had to let it go at that. Emil wrote a letter to Ernest, and told him of the rumors he had heard, and appealed to him as well as he could on paper. At best, that is a weak way to reach a person's heart.

Ernest answered Emil's letter. It was a long string of excuses for what he suspected his wife had written to them. But most of his letter was spent in maligning the whole truth of the Bible as they had learned and accepted it at Battle Creek College. They had loved it so much then, and the two of them had been baptized together in Lake Goguac. Dr. Ernest Huener went to great lengths to explain away the truth they had once loved. He said he had come to the conclusion that it was not necessary to observe any one certain day as the Sabbath, and he was not at all sure that the prophecies they used to believe applied to the present day at all. As to their living in the last days, he belittled the idea as absurd.

He sent Emil a book by a man named Canright, and some tracts written by a man named Ballenger.

"Don't read them, Emil," Jeanie had said in a low, tense voice. "If reading such stuff could make Ernest into the person he is today, and make him break his marriage vows, there is no good in them. You know the Bible says, 'By their fruits ye shall know them.' I don't care what

Ernest says; I know what we believe is true, and we are not living it as we should. And I have heard of that man Canright. Emil, when I was there he used to come around the office, and the brethren were so good to him. I know for a fact that he has been in and out of the church again and again. He is no authority.

"Before he left the last time, Emil, he came into the Review office, and he told one of the men he would come back if he could, but that it was too late. One time they told me they got him to attend a general meeting, and he was as pleased as a child. They said the old workers treated him most kindly, and that all through the meetings he laughed with tears in his eyes. They told us that he seemed to exist between two states of mind—uncontrollable joy and fearful, unassuaged grief."

"But Jeanie, I cannot reconcile that with some of this stuff he writes—if he felt that way, how could he have written some of this? I know for a fact that some of the stuff on only these first few pages is not true."

"Of course, Emil," Jeanie answered earnestly. "He does speak as if he believes it himself, but folks at Battle Creek say he knows he is telling lies, and that he is under a fearful and terrible conviction for what he has done."

"It is terrible if he did it for vindictiveness," Emil mused.

"That is exactly what he did it for," Jeanie said. "One of Canright's old friends told us of his talking to him in worship once. Canright said he wished the past could be blotted out and that he could be back in the work of God. He said Canright wept as he had never seen a man weep, and he kept moaning, 'I would be glad to come back, but oh, I cannot. It is too late. I am forever gone.' Later he told his friend that he must never fight the message he loved. That is enough for me," Jeanie added.

Emil seemingly assented, and Jeanie's fears were stilled; but later when she was in the barn looking after an old hen that had stolen her nest, she saw that Emil had been reading both books, for she saw them both on the table of the little room he used as an office where he kept his accounts. Old Hans had scoffed a lot, but Emil was carrying on his business correctly now, according to the book, and was prospering.

So IMPERCEPTIBLY that Jeanie hardly realized it at first, Emil began to change. He seldom touched his Bible, although they had pledged themselves that first year of their marriage to be one with God, and had asked Him to put a seal upon their happiness. Once when she mentioned it Emil had scoffed and said bitterly, "Oh, we were one with God all right—sure. Everything we had went up in smoke! That's what it cost to be one with God, Jeanie!"

"But Emil, to God—He—well, He will bring us hard things sometimes to purify us, and to bring us to our knees. And Emil, when our house burned, you know, we were drifting away from God, and going more and more after the dollar. You know that."

"I know we were digging in and trying our best to pay our honest debts," Emil had answered disagreeably. Then he had slammed out of the house, and Jeanie, looking after him, wondered where the joy had gone that had once been part and parcel of their lives. Even in the cabin they had known happiness, and they had often said that it was surely not material possessions that made for real contentment. Then Jeanie thought of Ernest, and of Carolyn and their little baby, and the unhappiness that had moved into their home, threatening its very foundations. Would unbelief, fostered and dallied with, do the same for Emil and her?

Little John's uncertain steps were taken on the floor of the log house. Emil would come home and see him clinging to the window sill, his round baby face alight at the joy of seeing daddy coming home. Dissatisfaction filled his heart. He looked around at the rooms that Jeanie had made so homelike, and he yearned bitterly for what had been. His determination to have done with the humility of living in a log house became an obsession. He talked it, he walked with it, and he even mumbled and muttered about it in his sleep. One night Jeanie was awakened by his blundering about the room, talking in such a loud tone that she knew he was walking in his sleep.

"Measure it off," he had shouted. "Measure it—forty feet—longest living room in the county. . . ."

"Emil, dear," she had said. "Emil—come back to bed."

He awakened and silently crept back into bed, but Jeanie knew he was planning big things in his heart; otherwise he would not dream them.

Things did not get any better, and Emil grew gruff and morose. Finally he began disregarding the edges of the Sabbath. At first it was, or seemed to be, an accident. One of the wheels came off the wagon while he was coming home from town on Friday afternoon. He had to unhitch and go all the way back to town, bareback, for help, and it was dark before he finally got home, where he found Jeanie very quiet and depressed. Supper had been ready and waiting so long on the back of the stove that it was a little dried, and the baby had been in his cradle for a long time.

Once the barriers were down, it began slowly to be the customary thing. Jeanie tried to carry on alone, and she remembered the Sabbath for a long time.

After a while it became terribly inconvenient to keep the Sabbath. It seemed that something would come up every week that made it extremely mandatory to carry on work as usual on God's day of worship. The threshing ring to which Emil belonged—well, when they had all turned up and worked so hard on his threshing, and had even threshed on Sunday because rain threatened, it didn't seem decent to take his teams and leave them in the lurch on Sabbath. He was distressed about it, though he did not let Jeanie know it. He salved his troubled conscience by telling himself that before another year he'd own his own threshing rig, or know the reason why, and then he could be the boss and call the strikes. He told Jeanie that it had to be done, for a man who did not support his family was worse than an infidel, and he had seen that in the Bible. Jeanie walked very quietly these days. Once the flood-gates were down, the enemy came in like a flood.

Emil seemed possessed with one consuming, driving desire—to make money, lots of it, and to climb back to the prestige he had enjoyed before the fire. It was hard to live in a cabin that folks in the county had raised out of pure pity when once he had owned what the newspaper said was the most beautifully appointed house for miles around. Now they were living like pioneers, with furniture hauled out of attics, outmoded and mismatched. The wound to his pride was an open sore.

WHEN JOHN was two May Rachel was born. The log house was full of baby things, and John graduated from the cradle to the trundle bed. Jeanie grew plumper and was more beautiful; she kept things up as she had done when they were alone. She canned and dried things from the large kitchen garden, of which she assumed full care. Emil had built a pantry onto the lean-to and dug a root cellar in the side of the hill. The pickling, preserving, and canning went on almost constantly from the time the first yellow transparent apple showed its bright plump self in the summer until the yellow pumpkins were rolled in and put into heaps in late October. A baby boy was born late in the fall of 1907. Emil named him Otto for pa's father in the old country, whom Emil faintly remembered. But something seemed to be wrong with the little fellow. He was never well. Jeanie worried almost to distraction—was up nearly every night with him. His little fingers were like bird's claws, and they clung pitifully to Emil's big thumb. His heart yearned over little Otto. As he looked down at the tiny frail form, he thought how little most folks realized how a helpless baby could appeal to a parent's heart. But oh, how he loved poor little Otto; and if he prayed any more at all, he sometimes said a prayer to God to give the baby the robust health that the other children enjoyed. He got up many a time in the night, when he heard the thin, piteous little wail and would walk the floor or rock the little fellow till he would fall into a restless, uneasy sleep.

John came down with the German measles when Otto was only three months old, and while he and May Rachel had them bad enough, and were cross and nauseated, it was nothing to what it did to the frail babe.

They saw with breaking hearts that he would never make the grade. Jeanie, weeping on Emil's shoulder as though her heart would break, told him how much she would like to bear the suffering if only the baby could rest and be healthy.

"Emil," she sobbed when neighbors were washing little Otto and dressing him for the small white casket that had been brought out from town, "Emil, maybe God wants us to—to—come back to Him. Maybe Otto's baby fingers will lead us back!"

But Emil did not answer. He only hardened his heart against a God who could take the baby from them. For days on end he could not speak to anyone without the tears streaming. Who would have dreamed that a babe so small could make such a tender place for himself in a father's heart?

Not long after little Otto was buried, Emil began work on a new barn. It was to be a gigantic affair, and old Hans was over every day, proud as punch of the elaborate plans, and at the heaps of fine materials arriving every day. And for it all, Emil proudly paid spot cash. He hired a regular carpenter to take charge of things, and he and pa helped as much as they could, along with the other work they were doing. Hans had kept his word and had not interfered with Emil, and now he seemed sort of mel-low, and took pride in the things Emil did, as if he had approved of all the book ways from the beginning. The barn, arising clean and massive, was the talk of the whole county. It was sixty-six feet square and sixty-five feet high. Emil walked around importantly and explained all about it to the visitors who came almost every day.

"Yes, sir," Jeanie heard him tell again and again, "it will hold 200 tons of mix and grain, 200 tons of hay, 100 head of cattle, 60 sheep, 15 horses, 15 to 20 hogs, and 300 hens."

One day during the building they had a frightful scare. John, who was five now, had a temper that threw him into such rages that unless they watched him, he might do bodily harm to himself or anything nearby. On this occasion something had provoked a fury of rage in the small boy, and Jeanie tried to get to him before he ran out the cabin door; but she was too late. Screaming at the top of his voice, he ran to the ladder that led to the rafters slowly rising in a skeletonlike framework and began climbing. From more than fifty feet up, he faced his frightened parents.

"I will jump," he shrilled. "I will jump if you don't let me have it! I will, Mamma. I will!"

Not knowing what else to do, they told him he could have the piece of cake, and he came down. But they both determined to curb the child before another such terrible crisis arose. So John paid dearly for the barn-climbing adventure and was the better boy for it. All Jeanie had to do when he began to indulge in a burst of temper was to go quietly and get the heavy razor strop, and he got sweet so suddenly that Jeanie was more than repaid for her firm stand on the matter.

Emil often talked about how advantageous having a fine barn was, and how it would be the means of making so much money that it would not be long until they could have a house that would be a regular show place.

But Jeanie knew that with all his bravado he was putting his money into a bag with holes in it, and that the Lord was not really blessing him. He made more money than anyone else in the county, but he had a lot of hard luck, too. The cholera struck his hogs, and Jeanie made brave enough to tell him that he knew better than to raise them in the first place. He did not answer that. Once he fell out of the mow and broke his right arm, and that took a lot of time and money. His best driving horse got to the corn one night and foundered and died. Then the well in the house yard dried up, and he had to drill another. He'd no sooner get one thing paid for than some other thing came up to worry the life out of him.

Another baby boy came to fill the aching void left by little Otto, and Emil began doggedly, almost angrily, to gather material together for a new house. Little John was trudging to school now, almost a mile away, and delighting his parents with the progress he made. Before Christmas he had read his primer through four times and was reading even the labels on the cans and spice tins. Jeanie was constantly telling ma about the things John did and said, and she hung on every word. Every minute she could spare she spent in the log house with Jeanie and the three babies. The new babe, husky from the first, was named Fritz, and Emil took a special fancy to him, almost as though he was trying to apologize for the weak frame of the lost Otto. He took him, crowing and appreciative, to the barn, even to the field, until Jeanie was nearly distracted with fear that something would happen to him; but ma only laughed.

"Don't fret ye, dear," she had said, a smile transforming her sad features. "If Hans had done that only once, my soul would have been fed. Emil has the tender soul and the loving heart. He will guard him with his life." And it was true. Fritz came back in his father's arms, rosy and smiling, even if he was often scandalously dirty. Jeanie need not have worried.

$\mathcal{T}$HE HEAPS OF FINE building supplies continued to grow. Emil would get a good buy on a quantity of hardwood, and it would be delivered and stored away. Pipes appeared, strong gleaming copper pipes, great cords of lath, seasoned hardwood for flooring or paneling or woodwork. In a short time he had cleared the knoll where the old house had stood, and he laid out the new one. It was to be brick veneer, three stories high. Jeanie need never be cramped in a log cabin again. He would do things up in great style. It would be the show place of the countryside. Strange to say, old Hans was as lifted up as Emil, and he appeared every day with hammer and a carpenter apron ma had secured for him. He worked as many hours as he could spare away from his forty acres. He seemed to have mellowed. One day Emil saw him pass by on his way home on top of a load of lumber. Consumed with curiosity, he and Jeanie went over that evening to see what was up.

They found ma, her face transformed and actually smiling as she held the lamp. Pa was tearing out the old antiquated kitchen cupboards. The dishes and the dry groceries were on chairs and tables.

"I ain't going to let a daughter-in-law of mine get ahead of ma," he tersely told Emil. But there was a twinkle in his old blue eyes. "I ain't so old but I can turn my hand to a thing or two myself, and we might as well have things a little handier here too."

Neighbors came for miles around to see the beautiful big house that Emil was building so strongly and so well. It seemed that he had thought of everything. That was a day when everyone used a zinc tub for the weekly bath, for few people dreamed of bathrooms. Yet Emil had seen the convenient bathrooms in the Battle Creek Sanitarium, and he determined that his house should have one, with the heating apparatus and all, no matter what it cost. It was put on the second floor, right across from Emil and Jeanie's bedroom.

Beneath the house was a full basement, equipped with bins for the root vegetables, a room for canned fruit, and floor space for storing the bounty of field and garden. The greatest marvel was a huge wood-burning furnace, which was to breathe warm air all over the house with a nominal amount of effort.

Emil was filled with pride over the beauty of his fine house, and even the newspapers featured it. They printed pictures of it, inside and out, with Emil proudly showing sightseers around. The only fly in his ointment was Jeanie. She was very quiet these days, and Emil was not a little disturbed with her lack of enthusiasm. He took it as a personal affront.

"Many a woman would think she was in heaven if she had what you are going to have," he said one day when he found her weeping as she sorted things in the little log house, preparatory to moving into the big show place.

"I know it," she said quietly.

"Well, what's wrong with you? What is it you do not like?" he had asked in such a loud voice that he reminded himself of Hans, his father.

"I did not say I did not like things, Emil," she told

him. "I do, and I know you are working almost beyond your strength. I wish you would take it a little easier. You are going to wreck your health."

"No, I won't," he said, a little kindlier. Then seeing she was putting all the things aside that she wanted to move into the new house, he demurred.

"Jeanie, let's throw all this stuff away. All of it. We have made good, and we can afford to start new."

"Not the cradle, Emil, not the trundle bed, and Emil, I like the dresser and the old spool bed. You mark my word, things like that will be more valuable than the cheap veneer stuff you buy now. They are solid and strong. They're still lovely."

"Well, as you please," he said, secretly feeling that Jeanie was a little old-fashioned. He wondered how the old stuff would look in the grand new house.

"We ought to be out of here in a week," he told her. "Then we can forget this disgraceful place ever existed."

"Disgraceful? Emil, I love every log of this house. We have had happiness here. All our children were born here, and little Otto died in my arms here by this fireplace. I can still see his sweet little face. And there is no disgrace in a struggle, Emil, and no disgrace even in a humble home, if there is love there, and if there is loyalty."

Emil looked at her a moment, then turned and went out to the great monument he was building to his pride. He knew what she meant. He knew in his heart that they had lost some of the sweetness of their lives together when he lost his faith. Their old comradeship became only a memory when he got to making money hand over fist, until there did not seem to be time to do the things they had loved so much in the early days of their married life—reading together; hitching up, and attending the little crossroads church on prayer meeting night; giving Bible studies to neighbors, to the current hired man; long walks on the Sabbath, and studying the Sabbath school lessons together.

JEANIE THOUGHT RUEFULLY that she really should be the happiest matron in that part of the country. The floors of the house were of different kinds of hardwood—oak, walnut, cherry, and hickory. The great winding staircase leading up from the entrance hall was bird's-eye maple. Emil walked like a king. He had the finest barn and the finest house in the whole countryside. Finally they were moved in, and Jeanie had plenty of room to store her treasures. Emil's furniture bill for his first house was as nothing compared with what it cost to furnish this giant of a house. He laughed a little at remembering how worried and upset he was at owing such a big bill, and how hard he had struggled to get it paid, only to have the work of many months go up in flames in a few minutes. He thought of the organ, of the violin, and of the magic lantern. He thought of all the wedding presents and the keepsakes that Jeanie had lost. His heart smote him a little, for he had not been as kind and as considerate as he should be. He had caught himself lately being more like pa than he ever wanted to be. He would change, he would, and show Jeanie that he still loved her. He would capture anew the old joy and the breathless ecstasy of the companionship he had bartered away in the mad rush to make money and to make lots of it. He would—but Emil did not realize that you cannot sell your birthright and then have it back again for the mere asking. You cannot revive a fragile and living thing that a harsh boot has crushed ruthlessly into the ground. That is one thing he could not know, but clumsily he began to try, and Jeanie was touched and grieved over the failure in her heart to join his eager quest for the joy he longed for. She well knew it could never be had till he began to believe again with a simple childlike trust. Ernest and Carolyn had been separated for several years. Carolyn was practicing medicine on the West Coast, and Ernest was about to break up. Without faith, there was no happiness, Jeanie told herself, and Emil had fed his skepticism so long that the road back would be exceedingly hard. In her discouragement even Jeanie had gone the way of least resistance and had long since quit even a semblance of keeping the Sabbath. The feeling of uneasiness never left her heart, however, and try as she might, she could never get away from it.

Once in the new house, Emil set to work so grimly that every debt was paid off within a year's time. Jeanie was drawing a big batch of bread out of the oven one fall day when he came in and threw down all the paid notes on the table in front of her. After greasing the tops of the fragrant brown loaves, she picked the papers up to see what he had brought. To him it meant they had virtually arrived. And it ought to mean the same thing to Jeanie.

"Oh, Emil," she cried, "this is wonderful. And you have worked so hard. Now you can take it a little easier, though the care of this house will always be great. I hate to have a hired girl all the time."

"Think nothing about it," Emil said expansively. "I would not expect you to keep it clean and do all the work by yourself. This is no cabin."

"No, honey," she said, "but we were so happy in our cabin—little John and the babies."

"They can be happier here," he said firmly. "Now, Jeanie, I have brought you something for a celebration. Ought we not to celebrate our being free from debt?"

"Why, honey, it is enough for me to know you have all these big debts paid. That is celebration enough."

"Not enough for me," Emil cried, and the look on his face was so eager it was pathetic. He was a person who wanted to eat his cake and have it too.

Taking her by the arm, he led her into the big living room at the front of the house. How he got it in without her hearing the noise, Jeanie could not imagine, but there it was, as lovely a piano as she ever laid her eyes on. It was a German make, a Hinsman. The case was of polished Circassian walnut; it was the most beautiful instrument Jeanie had ever seen. And beside it, lying on the parlor table, was a fine violin in a black case lined with purple plush.

"Play it! Play it!" he cried, pulling her to the lovely thing, which strangely enough, she was reluctant to touch.

Seating herself, she put her unaccustomed fingers on the white keys. What should she play? Almost as if someone else placed her fingers, she began to play:

"My faith looks up to Thee,
    Thou Lamb of Calvary . . ."

Emil did not say a word, but stood gazing out of the west window, his face looking so old and so sad that Jeanie's heart smote her. But how could she play and sing as she used to, when the music had gone out of her soul?

Jeanie began to go to a popular church in the neighborhood. Emil went with her occasionally, and she knew why—it was good business. She had heard the phrase so many times that she almost loathed it—making of church-going a mercantile thing. Yet she wanted the children to go to church—if only for the respectability of the thing, and for the good company they would be likely to meet in such a place. It was strange to think they could ever do a thing like that—they who had once "borne the vessels of the Lord"; they who had once learned to know and to love the doctrine of the Sabbath of the Lord, and who had looked eagerly for His soon appearing in the clouds of heaven.

MA DIED ONE winter night without even having been sick. Emil had dreaded to go to see her, though she never had said a word to him to chide or to scold him. Emil used to think he could tell what she was thinking, though. Her old hands, almost transparent, used to tremble violently whenever the subject of the Sabbath or the coming of the Lord was mentioned. She had never been the same since Ernest's trouble. Emil had seen the light go out of her eyes. And she seemed to get feeble overnight.

The day after her funeral pa came over, and he was gentler than he had ever been. He acted as though he wanted to talk to someone about ma. It was as though he had bartered his days of warmth away in the market place of greed, and now cold, he was trying to warm himself by embers long stark and cold. They stood looking out on the lovely patchwork quilt made by the beautiful fields of Emil's farm.

"She kept it, Emil."

"Kept what, Pa?" Emil asked gently.

"Why, the Sabbath, Emil. Not like I have—no. That was no good, Emil, even though the day is right; but I did not keep it because of that. I kept it because—well, never mind that; it is so much water under an old bridge, but ma was never as I was. She was timid, and I—I wasn't always as good to her as I ought to have been."

Emil was amazed to see hard-wrung tears squeezing from his father's faded-blue eyes. Harsh old eyes they were, like icy pools edged with briers. His mouth trembled pitifully.

"You were good to ma lately, Pa," Emil was constrained to say kindly. "Ma told me she wished she had had such a nice handy house when she was rearing us children. You made the house so handy and so neat."

"I was fifty years late," he said, his voice weak and quavering. "I had made out to tell her, too, that I wished I had done things to make it easy for her. But words like that are hard for me to say. I have said the other kind so much that my tongue has forgotten how to be gentle."

"Ma knew, Pa. She told me you had been good to her in fixing things up so nice." Emil did not tell him that ma had said pa had never before in all their years together been so good and thoughtful.

"Yes, but if only I could have told her. Now it is too late. Don't you get into habits like mine, Emil, where it is easier to say a hateful word than to say a civil one. Don'cha do it, Emil. There ain't nothin' so hard to bear as to owe a debt, to have the money to pay it and ye can't do it no way." He went walking off down the road so slowly and so feebly that it was hard for Emil to realize that it was arrogant, loud-spoken old pa who had been talking to him.

Their fields were full of the finest stock, the barn was loaded with grain, and fine cattle and horses stood in the stalls. Everywhere were lavish evidences of great prosperity.

And because Emil and Jeanie had not received the love of the truth, they were in the throes of the great delusion spoken of in the Bible, that they who reject God's counsels will eventually believe a lie.

IT DID NOT happen suddenly, oh, no. Things like that creep up on a person so slowly and so insidiously that the change is almost imperceptible. Day by day of self-seeking and neglect of God's requirements, day after day of looking after things that may seem all-important, but which will be as wood, hay, and stubble in the final judgment, and the heart becomes callous where once was tenderness, even to the point of loving those things once despised and feared.

It seems almost incredible that Jeanie, who had gone to minister to the poor in the missions of Chicago, Jeanie, who had prayed at the bedside of her patients, and who had seen many a one find Christ through the maze of searing pain and looming shadow—that she should join the great popular church in the town. Oh, no, it did not come in a day or a week or a year. But once, when Jeanie was teaching a Sunday school class, such a qualm of realization came over her that she had to stop teaching in the middle of the lesson and sit down, and people said she had some kind of faint or seizure.

Without neglecting her reputation as a good mother and neighbor, Jeanie worked hard for the good of the community. She was efficient as leader of the Women's Club and as a member of the Eastern Star. People could not say enough good things about her, or about Emil either, for that matter. He was looked up to as the biggest stockman in the country, and a Midas for making money. It seemed that everything he touched turned to gold.

Then, as if the devil would have his way more perfectly, discord came and lived with them. They both worked too hard and were on the go too much, and being too weary, they took it out on each other. Violent quarrels, which at first surprised and hurt both of them, gave vent to hateful and ugly words that poured out like a flood, until neither of them could be the same again. Both would remember all their lives the searing words shouted in moments of anger.

They were swiftly changing their pretty home into a place which the children would never remember without mixed feelings. Expenditures were lavish, too lavish. Then if the money to pay for some extravagance seemed to come in a little slowly, each would blame the other.

Emil knew well from long experience that Jeanie had an astute and shrewd head for business, and he would make no major decisions without her sanction. He would insist on her passing judgment on some matter of great importance. If it came to good and they prospered, which was often the case, he said nothing of it and did not acknowledge her help in turning the transaction in their favor. But woe be if she did not give the wisest counsel in all things. If something went askew, she would hear of it and be reminded of it in loud, censorious tones. "But Emil," she would protest, hurt to the quick, "I told you to sell the yearlings to Borden, as he gave you the first and the best offer and would be more likely to repeat. I told you that if Bennett did offer you a better price, he would not repeat, and he would not be so likely to pay promptly. I——"

"You told me Bennett, and I can prove it by Ole, who was standing there; and I can prove it by——"

"No, you can't, Emil," Jeanie said quietly. "Ole was

in town. He was not there at all, and I did not tell you Bennett. I never did favor——"

"You did, and you are trying to crawfish; you always do when things go wrong. Before I ask you anything again——"

"I will take it as a favor, Emil, if you do not," Jeanie answered, so angry that her voice trembled. "You decide everything yourself, and see where it gets you."

"I will," he shouted. "I will. We owe all our hard luck to your so-called brilliant decisions."

"We do?" Jeanie cried, outraged at the injustice of his words. "Who gave you that tip about the Clayton Creamery? We cleared a lot of money on that, and you said yourself it would have been impossible if I hadn't been on my toes. And who told you about Jarrett's putting up the steers for sale? I——"

But Emil had slammed out of the house, sick at heart in spite of his bluster, for he knew he was not telling the truth or doing right; and he could not seem to do any different. It was strange, but every once in a while Bible verses he had learned in the dear dead years gone by came up like ghosts to point accusatory fingers at him.

"What I would, that do I not; but what I hate, that do I," he thought, his heart burning with the remorse he always felt at the look Jeanie gave him when he was particularly unjust.

95

But in stubbornness he knew he was like old pa, and hating himself, he would make his own decisions and would get into a worse muddle than before. Usually Jeanie would not retaliate, and he was grateful that she was not like him, blaming everyone but himself when reverses came. But on a later occasion she lost her usual composure, and the scars of that bitter afternoon would never be erased.

"This is one of your wise decisions," she scathingly pointed out. "Oh, yes, you said you would not ask my opinion any more; you said you would decide for yourself. Well—I told you you would lose if you did it this way. But no, you never make mistakes!"

ᗷITTER WORDS. HATEFUL words. Emil hated himself for stirring them up, and sometimes he hated life so much he wished he were dead. Jeanie moved sullenly about the beautiful house, and if she ever dreamed, it was of the dear days when she and Emil and the babies had been so happy in the cabin. Once after an altercation Jeanie moved out of the big room they had shared, and she put all her things in a guest room. She was still doing the accounts for the farm, so she exchanged the double bed for a single one and put in a desk and shelves for her files. She and her husband became almost strangers in the great house. Jeanie did so much work for the dairy, the stock business, and the dozen other enterprises Emil had going, that a hired girl was employed, and Jeanie did her share of the money-making. In spite of Emil's frequent bursts of anger at her, he realized that she had more business acumen than most people, and he relied on her more than he himself realized. They established a sort of armed truce and went in for profits on a big scale.

"Emil," she said one night, when they were finishing supper in the great dining room, "let's go in for potatoes. Let's grow them and buy all that our neighbors raise. Let's build a place to store them and have a potato exchange for the district. We grow really fine potatoes here, and I believe that if we worked it right, we could get top market prices. I was thinking the other day of how the city buyers swarm out here in the spring and try to bargain for our output. Well, if they get a rakeoff, why can't we?"

Emil looked at her for a moment without answering. She was as smart as mustard, and he realized it. Why had he not thought of that before?

"I believe you are as right as rain, Jeanie," he said. He finished his apple pie, and without a word he went out and looked at the old barn he had left standing when he built the new one. It was sturdy, having been built of good strong wood, and he had kept his buildings in repair. It would cost money to fix it so potatoes would not freeze, but he was sure there was real money in a venture like that.

Jeanie smiled as she went about the work of helping the girl get things readied up for the night. The children were in the sitting room, and Jeanie made them all study some of an evening.

May Rachel was ten and Fritz was seven. John was thirteen and was growing tall and apple-cheeked as Emil had been. May Rachel was a silent girl, and one often wondered what she was thinking. She got high grades in school, but was so quiet and uncommunicative that Jeanie was provoked. She wore her lovely brown hair braided and wound around her head. She did not seem to take to fancy things as Jeanie would have liked. Anything frivolous she would accept gravely and thank the giver. But then she would put it away, and no one could prevail on her to use or wear it.

"I think you might wear that ruffled dress Aunt Nettie went to all the trouble to make for you, May," mother would begin.

"It was very kind of Aunt Nettie," May Rachel would answer, but then she would go away to her room and say no more. What could you do with a girl like that? She practiced long hours on the piano, and Jeanie got her the best teacher in town. But her interest lay more in books and reading. Jeanie would give the child chores to do to keep her from having her head in a book all the time. She would work sweetly, patiently, and efficiently, and then go back to her book again.

The house was so big that each one had a room of his own. Fritz's room was next to his mother's, and May Rachel's was at the corner. It was furnished in bird's-eye maple and flowered chintz curtains. Emil chose his in the tower of the third floor. The hired girl slept in the bedroom that opened off the kitchen. Every morning her singing in German while she built the kitchen fire was the signal for all to get up.

John graduated that year from the eighth grade in the country school. His father told him he could have a horse to ride to attend high school in town. Grandpa, old and feeble, happened to be in the barn when Emil told the lad that.

Habits of a lifetime are hard to break, and old grandpa, bent as a horseshoe, tried to demur and to tell Emil he would be the ruination of the boy if he coddled him like that, and that education was not the key to heaven by any means. But Emil's voice was as decisive as a surgeon's knife.

"Oh, no, Pa," he answered as gently as the clipped words would allow. "I don't want John to make the mistake I made. My children are going to have all the education they're a mind to have."

"You got along, didn't ye?" the old man queried,

slyly, a glint of triumph in his old eyes. "You could buy and sell any neighbor 'round here. You ain't never worsened yourself by givin' up yer schooling."

But Emil was in no mood for family diplomacy tonight. His soul was bared in the ugly glare of reality.

"Maybe I did, Pa," he answered shortly. "There is something about a man's peace of mind that is worth something, too. And that I have not got."

Grandpa hurried away, muttering to himself, and Emil knew in his heart that his old father did not have it either.

THE POTATO EXCHANGE that Jeanie had suggested succeeded in such proportions that Emil did an unprecedented thing. He did not even tell Jeanie, for she would have opposed it—he was sure of that. He went in to the high school and got John out and talked to him long and earnestly. He couldn't have done it at home without arousing Jeanie's suspicions.

"Listen, son," he told the lad when he got him outside. "I hate to mention this, for I may be making a mistake, and I know that mother would object, but we are making a mint of money out of potatoes, and we need you right now like everything. I must hire someone, and you could make some easy money that would help you out later on. Just drop out of school the rest of this year and you can earn enough to take up any profession you want."

John stood there and considered. It would mean losing half a year of school, but he was ahead of most of them anyhow, and he might even study and keep up. He felt sure in his heart that he could do both, and he resolved to give it a try.

Jeanie bitterly opposed John's leaving school, as he knew she would. He heard his parents quarreling late in the night about it, and he could not sleep for the turbulence that seemed to fill the house. He noticed at breakfast that his mother's eyes were almost swollen shut from her weeping. As soon as the meal was over, he took her aside.

"Listen, Mother," he said, holding her trembling hands in his. "Now you just listen to me and don't interrupt till you hear what I have to say, and you will see it is not as bad as you think it is."

She buried her face in her son's shoulder and began to sob anew. John put his arm around her and tried to comfort her.

She clung to John so disconsolately that his heart was touched, and he had a notion to go tell dad that he would not leave school. She finally controlled her hard, tearing sobs.

"Mother," he began, still holding to her hand, "you

know that I have been getting good grades, the top grades in the class. Now, I am going up and ask the principal to let me study at home and take the exams, and I won't miss a thing. You will see, I will make it, and I'm sure I can make money too. Mother, I am of a mind to be a great man someday, and I want you to be proud of me so you can say, 'That man is my son.' I want to go to college and to the State university, and that takes a lot of money. I believe I can make a lot at this potato game. After all, Mother, don't forget, it was your brain storm."

She smiled a little wanly at this, and John knew he had her in hand and had touched a little on her pride. He was sorry that dad did not always give her credit for the successes for which she really deserved the praise. Instead, he always ragged the life out of her if something went wrong, but said not a word when everything was coming their way. Things were not right at home, and John knew it, but he did not know what was wrong. He did not know that his mother had leaned over the cradle in the log house and said to Emil, "Oh, Emil, dear; isn't the baby just too beautiful? Let us dedicate him to the Lord, Emil, as Hannah did Samuel. Won't it be wonderful to have our son be a worker for God?"

So John did not know that he had been given to the Lord. And the pity of it was that Jeanie seemed to have forgotten the momentous thing too, for precious little of the beauty of truth did the children find in their home life. It was grind, grind, and grind some more, and work till the night grew still, for if Emil earned a thousand at one game, he was as eager for the second thousand as he was for the first.

Young John, strong and alert, did just as he promised Jeanie. He worked like a slave all day, and it seemed as if everything turned to gold under his eager efforts. His presence in the office and at the big storage barns freed Jeanie somewhat, and she had more leisure than she had had for years, and John seemed to possess the same acumen and good judgment that she had. Emil consulted him about everything.

They made thousands at the potato pool, and a crop failure in another part of the country skyrocketed prices, so everyone in the county was pleased because they had received more for their potatoes than ever before.

At John's suggestion they bought up cattle and fed and fattened them for sale. It was a way, John reasoned, to use up the vast supplies of surplus feed that fairly bulged their gigantic barn. And it gave them a greater profit than selling the feed.

MEANWHILE JEANIE JOINED several new clubs and was a social leader in the town. She was the president of the local Women's Club and she sang in the choir at the Presbyterian church. The three churches in town combined for Sunday school, and she taught one of the Sunday school classes. Yes, Jeanie forgot what God explicitly adjured His children to remember; and she who had gone with Dr. David Paulson and his group to preach Christ on the South Side of Chicago had sold the truth she once loved so dearly. Her conscience, seared with a hot iron, was not wrenched at the thought that her children were being reared without it. Their birthright was denied them.

Right in the midst of the Huener prosperity America entered World War I. Then they really did make money. But they lost money too. And in the dead of winter the terrible influenza epidemic struck. Doc Peters stopped one night to warm his feet. He had been stuck in the snow on his way to a lonely farm.

Mother had him stay to eat some of her good vegetable soup, so warm and filling, and she had a "war cake," made with a great economy of sugar, shortening, and white flour; and it was good. The rest of the family had eaten, so mother and John sat at the dining table to keep the doctor company while he ate.

"Oh, if we only had more nurses," he fairly groaned. "I believe we could save more lives, but as it is they are dying—yes, dying, Mrs. Huener, like flies."

John saw his mother's eyes light up as they had not done in years.

"Dr. Peters," mother said, "I am a graduate nurse —a graduate of the Battle Creek School of Nursing."

"What?" Dr. Peters leaped to his feet so suddenly that he almost upset his tall glass of milk. "Are you a nurse, Mrs. Huener? If you are you must help me. With a woman of your mettle we can save lives all over the county. Why, you could be the answer to my prayers, and don't say you won't go! Don't!"

"I will go with you, Dr. Peters," mother answered. "I have felt condemned for some time for not using my profession, especially since so many are so ill and so few know how to take care of the sick. It has been some time— well, it has been fifteen years since I nursed, but I guess it is something a person never forgets.

"You're right, Mrs. Huener, especially a Battle Creek nurse. They have a reputation known all over the world, and if you will help me——"

"When do you need me?" mother asked.

"Now, right now, tonight!" Dr. Peters pleaded urgently. "Can you get your things and come with me right now? Do you have someone to carry on here?"

"Oh, yes," mother laughed easily. "I have had a woman helping me for some time, since I help Emil so much, and she can manage. I'll run and get my things. My nursing suitcase is packed away in a closet on the third floor. Run and get it, Emil, while I pack a bag. I'll be with you in twenty minutes, doctor."

The influenza epidemic was serious, and it did not take Jeanie long to find her nursing uniform, packed away for so long in a closet on the third floor, and start on her rounds of mercy with old Dr. Peters.

"Bert Sipes's oldest girl is down sick, Mrs. Huener, and you know they lost their mother at the beginning of the epidemic. If Molly dies, I don't know what will become of those little motherless children, with Bert the triflin' drunk he is and has been. I am going to take you right there."

So JEANIE BEGAN again. At first it was a little strange, and she had to get back into a routine, but it did not take her a day. She had wrapped her old uniforms up and had them in a trunk that had not been burned in the fire. They were a bit yellow, but as pretty as ever, though some might have said they were out of style. She did have to shorten all the skirts, for they were at least a foot longer than anyone wore at that time.

From that day onward Dr. Peters was the most sought-after physician in the county. The news got out that he did not lose a case. He was on the go day and night, till he fairly seemed to sleep while he was walking. But to one and all he declared that he did not deserve all the credit.

"You've got to hand it to Jeanie Huener," he told the townspeople. "I'd have lost several if it hadn't been for her. I tell you, you never saw the beat of it. Don't need medicine with Jeanie around. We have hardly to arrive in a house before she'll have a boiler of water on, and the way she goes after usin' those pieces of wool blanket—she calls 'em hydro-fomentations, or something of the kind. But they beat all the medicine in the drugstore. She'll get right after the stuff they eat, too, and have them drinkin' lemonade sweetened with honey, and sassafras tea, and not a lick of meat will she let them have."

"You don't mean it, doc," someone would answer incredulously. "It's a wonder they could keep up their stren'th, not feedin' 'em good strong meat to build 'em up like that."

"Yes, but you ought to hear her tell about that," doc laughed, long and comfortably. "She wrote me out something that Doc Kellogg wrote, when I was trying to tell her that a little bacon and ham wouldn't do the patient any hurt. Let's see if I have it somewhere."

And he dug around in his pocket till he found a neatly written quotation and read it aloud to his friend.

" 'Fruits without doubt formed a leading constituent, perhaps the leading element, in the original bill of fare of the human race. Recent bacteriological investigations have shown clearly that those microorganisms which are most abundant in most forms of indigestion, particularly those accompanied by so-called biliousness, coated tongue, et cetera, do not thrive in any kind of fruit juice and die quickly in grape juice. This fact shows quite conclusively the great value of a fruit dietary in disease.' "

"You know, it is funny, Jake," he said. "One of

108

Jeanie's patients rebelled and said he had had his coffee and bacon all his life and no nurse was going to tell him he had to live on bananas and fruit like a chimpanzee. Well, we almost lost that feller, and let me tell you, he came to the fruit diet in a hurry, and was glad to. And today he'd deed his farm to Mrs. Huener, he is so grateful."

WHILE JEANIE was nursing, running to and fro in the county, and happier than she had been in years, John and Emil were fairly coining money. It was nothing to make a profit of three hundred dollars in a day. Then spring came, the epidemic let up, and Jeanie came home. John took his examinations and graduated with his class.

He made an oration and was gratified to see in the audience his mother and father, his brother, Fritz, and May Rachel, his sister. They had been far from being a closely knit family. He hardly knew Fritz who had been in grade school while he was in high school. May Rachel was just a kid who got in the way and tattled on him. Now, looking at them, he had a pang of regret, for he wished he had done a little differently with his life.

His oration, "Rome Was Not Built in a Day," he delivered with all the force and expression he could muster, as he had learned in Professor Harroth's class in vocal expression. Mother beamed as he made his graceful gestures and struck his well-learned attitudes. She was conscious that everyone must be envying her the possessing of such a bright and gifted boy.

Then he went home and helped father for the summer. He sent in his application to a college in a nearby town, intending to major in English and business. That way he would not have all his eggs in one basket. If he decided to teach he could, and if he wanted to enter business he could do that too.

He boarded at the college town during the week, but on Friday he came home and helped his father. Once he skipped classes on Thursday and Friday and took a large shipment of potatoes to Detroit, which netted the family several thousand dollars. He was becoming very sure of himself. He felt all kinds of contempt for the poor lugs who did not seem to be able to make out. Why, he had money for everything he wanted, and he felt sure that anyone who used his brains could do the same.

Then suddenly John became aware of the fact that mother was not very well. It was nothing he could put his finger on, but she just did not seem like mother. More often than not, she was lying down when he came home.

"Mother, what's the matter?" he would ask.

"Oh, nothing, dear. I am all right. How did school go this week? What did you do?"

"I got along fine, Mother, but does dad know you are not feeling well? Have you been to the doctor?"

"John, I am just tired. I made strudel today, for you know Hilda never makes it to suit father. I finished up a dress for May Rachel. She is in a class play and she seems to think she has nothing to wear."

So she would pass it off, but John could tell that she was not well, and he worried about her. But most of the time he was in high spirits. He felt sure he was on the high road to success, and it was a bright and shining goal just ahead, almost within reach. His teachers hinted of openings for young men of his caliber, and dad spoke seriously of his becoming his junior partner.

"If you marry, son, some years from now, you can build on the hill back on the other side of the woods. Your mother wanted this house to go there, but somehow I wanted it where the old one had been. I guess I insisted on my way too much, for mother does not seem too happy."

"Maybe you did, Dad, but I don't think mother is too well. She is not like she was at all, and she is a lot thinner. I think you ought to see a doctor."

MARY, JEANIE'S SISTER, had gone to the sanitarium at Mount Vernon, Ohio, after Jeanie and Emil had married and left Battle Creek. Mary had noted with pained interest the steady decline of the spirituality of the little family and had deplored it. She spoke her mind so to the point that Jeanie, not a little nettled, quit writing to her, and a time or two sent Mary's letters back unopened. But lately Mary had been up to something else. She had taken to sending the children *Our Little Friend* and *The Youth's Instructor*, religious papers that Jeanie had read and loved when she was a young girl, and the children were delighted with them. Fritz was usually out to the mailbox eagerly waiting for the mailman on Thursday, the day the papers usually arrived.

Jeanie felt condemned to see this, for she knew down in her heart that they would have delighted in a childhood such as they should have had if she and Emil had been faithful. But now it seemed to be too late. Jeanie knew that Mary must be the one who was sending the things, for who in the world but Mary would take the trouble to do so? It worried her not a little.

Then, as if that were not enough, a magazine began to arrive addressed to her. It was the *Canadian Watchman*, and for a while she laid it away and did not read it. But her curiosity, or was it an old hunger, got the better of her, and she began to read it from cover to cover every week—secretly, though, for she did not want anyone to see her. But she began to await the coming of the *Watchman* with the same eagerness that May Rachel and Fritz looked for their papers.

ONE FRIDAY AFTERNOON when John arrived home mother had been put to bed officially, and a nurse in a snowy starched uniform was presiding over the sickroom. His fears were realized. Mother was seriously ill, though even the doctor could not lay his finger on the trouble. He said it was nerves, but John suspected it was more of the heart and the spirit than a sickness of the body. He knew that she was sad all the time, and he blamed his father and his thoughtless brusqueness and loud faultfinding for a lot of it. Mother was made of more delicate fiber than his dad, and she couldn't take the constant bickering and complaining that had gradually undermined her health. He longed for an opportunity to put it up to dad, for he was sure he did not realize how rude and hateful he had been with her, and how it sounded to the children.

Of course, John had no idea of the background of belief his mother and father had left ruthlessly behind in their mad fervor for money-making, nor could he realize how the unbearable pangs of a conscience long-violated had been taking their terrible toll of his mother's health and spirit.

When he went in to see her, she tried to smile and reassure him that all was well; and he bent down to kiss her. Suddenly she drew away from him and burst

8 113

into uncontrollable weeping. The nurse came running, but Jeanie waved her away. John was amazed. He vaguely realized that he was the cause of this outburst, but was hard put to find out what he had done.

"Mother," he cried, kneeling by the bed and putting his arm under her pillow. "Mother, darling, what have I done? I wouldn't hurt you. I'd cut off my arm first."

It was quite a while before she could tell him the reason for her tears. Finally he found out. It was the smell of tobacco on his breath that made her know for a surety that he was smoking. He had tried to keep it from her, for he knew that she didn't like it, but he had no idea she felt so strongly, or he wouldn't have started it in the first place. It had not meant that much to him.

"Oh, John," she wailed, "it is those terrible cigarettes. Honey, at Battle Creek we learned so much about what they would do to a person's body and mind. Now to have you smoking seems as if it will kill me. I know it has been my fault. I have not taught you as I ought to have done, or this thing would never have happened."

With this the sobs began again, and they shook her frail frame so terribly that John was alarmed. He could only dimly get the point of what she was trying to tell him, for the idea that smoking was wrong had not occurred to him. He patted her hand awkwardly.

"I can quit any day I want to, Mother," he told her. "It hasn't got the hold on me that it has on some fellows, and I will quit—that's what I will do; I will show you I can. I won't smoke any more."

To prove his point he took the two packs of cigarettes he had with him at the moment and laid them on the little fire that was burning in her bedroom grate. "I will never touch another cigarette, for your sake, Mother," he said tenderly, noting with alarm how thin she had become. He was ashamed that he had not noticed before. Mother was someone you just took for granted, and he could hardly imagine life without her. Nonetheless, a bell of alarm rang in his heart. His mother did not seem as assured as he had wanted her to be. The worried and anxious look did not leave her face.

"John, dear," she said tenderly, "it is not as easy as that. Once they get a hold on you, it takes great strength of character and will power to conquer the habit. I know, for I have seen smokers struggle, when they had a heart condition and the doctor told them that they either had to give up the habit or face alarming results. I have heard men say they would rather face death than undergo the misery of giving up the tobacco habit. Honey, it is not as easy as you think."

John looked down at her. He had heard so little of her life before she had met dad. Sometimes he had wondered why both dad and his mother shut up like a couple of clams whenever anything came up about their earlier lives.

115

"Mother," he answered, smiling at her and patting her hand, "don't get the least bit worried as to me. I tell you, I have never let it get the hold on me that some fellows have. It's nothing. I won't even miss it. I just smoked because the rest did, and I guess—well, I guess I thought it was the smart thing to do. Don't give it another thought. I am quitting for keeps, and that's that."

"I am glad, dear," Jeanie said, smiling up at him, and inwardly rejoicing that he was not of a stubborn turn of mind, for she knew of many a boy who would not so readily do as his mother wanted, without arguments, scenes, or a hateful defiance. He had ever been kind and thoughtful of her, and she had taken a great deal of comfort in him—more than he could have known.

ᛒUT JUST as he was about to leave the room she asked him to get her a magazine that she had been reading and which she had put on a table in the hall. He went and hunted it out and gave it to her. It was a *Canadian Watchman*. She leafed through it and then came to an article on cigarette smoking, and she handed it to her son.

"Just in case," she said. "Just in case you have a bad time, here is a fine article on curing yourself, and it was written by a man that I knew when I was in Battle

Creek. He and his wife were both doctors, and I had a great deal of respect for them. You take it to your room, and if you need it you will have it."

John laughed at her, but he took the paper with the article in it by a Dr. Daniel H. Kress, on how to cure the cigarette habit.

He read the first paragraph as he stood there, his mother watching anxiously.

"The first step in giving up the cigarette is to give it up. This must be done, after counting the cost, and regardless of the circumstances. Many fail because they never reach this point."

He scanned down the page, partly from curiosity and partly to please his mother, for he considered the whole thing a tempest in a teapot. How could a thing like that get the hold on him to warrant all this fuss? There were references to getting some gentian root or camomile blossoms, and chewing them during the day when the desire to smoke becomes overwhelming. Rochelle salts and cream of tartar were recommended every morning for a week to help eliminate the poison. Then there were a lot of things said about eating meat and hot seasonings, and the advisability of eating a lot of fresh fruits while breaking the habit.

"All right, Mother," he told her. "I will take this, and if I need it I will surely use it; but I do not think I will have a bit of trouble."

As he was leaving, John noticed his mother looked so sad, so unutterably sorrowful, that he was constrained to ask her again what was troubling her. He felt that all was not well, but he could hardly put his hand on just what was wrong.

"I am not doing right, John. I have gone against my conscience for a long time, and I wonder whether the Lord can ever forgive me. I knew better than to live as I have been doing."

"What, Mother?" John asked curiously. He could not imagine his dear kind mother as being anything else but a wondrously clever and good woman.

"I want to tell you, John," she answered. "There are so many things I want you to know, for somehow I have a feeling that I may not live too long. And I must tell you a lot of things I should have told you a long, long time ago. I have sinned in not living as I should. I have owed it to you children to rear you differently. I see it now."

John kissed his mother again and left, wondering greatly.

TO JOHN'S AMAZEMENT, leaving off the cigarettes was not the snap he had thought it would be. He had no idea the thing held him so tightly in its clutches. He had enough of his mother's make-up to detest weakness and he hated himself for sitting in rhetoric and biology and European history and being able to think of nothing but cigarettes. While Professor Crabbe was discussing the lightning career of the Little Corsican, all he could think of was "Well, in just forty-one minutes this class will be over. I will have four and a half minutes to get to biology—but I think I can run across to Bauer's store, buy a pack, and get a pull or two before the bell rings."

Then he remembered his solemn promise to his mother. He recalled how he had laughed at the thought that he would need to have anything to help him break away from what seemed to be a pleasant and harmless pastime. He was furious that he could not keep his mind on his lesson, or think of anything else except the longing in every pore of his body for the detestable little white tubes of which he had been so sure he was the master. But he was not, and it was with a sense of despair that he acknowledged it to himself.

Only that morning his mother had asked him to bring her Bible, and she had read a text to him. She repeated it several times and asked him to say it again and again to her. He did it to humor her, for he was sure she knew that he was having a struggle. She told him, too, that breaking any habit was never as easy as he had imagined. The text was to the point, too. You had to hand it to mother. She could see right through a fellow.

"For of whom a man is overcome, of the same is he brought in bondage." Bondage? What man of any character at all would want to be a slave? He fairly gritted his teeth and whispered under his breath, "I will *not* smoke again—I will *not*—I will *not*. I won't be a slave to a crazy little thing not four inches long, no bigger around than a pencil. It is ridiculous—I won't do it!"

GRIMLY HE SET about to free himself, for he was enslaved, and he realized it now. But he would be free—he would. He went to the drugstore and got the gentian root—but he was infuriated when several of the fellows, suspecting that he was trying to quit, set about to tempt him.

"Have a cigarette, John," one of them said, almost too casually, as he was emerging from the gymnasium.

"Nope," John had replied, not even looking at the proffered gift, which every fiber of his being cried out for. He could hardly keep from seizing it, but he steeled himself against the wild conflict going on inside him. "Nope, I don't want it."

"You do so," taunted the other. "You want it so badly that you would burn for it."

"That may be," retorted John. "You have said it—

just about—well, I guess I feel partly that way. But I am going to show you fellows that I am strong enough to battle off a thing like that. I don't believe that one of you is strong enough to quit—if you *wanted* to. I happen to want to, and I am going to quit."

"Oh, we could so, *if* we wanted to," was one easy rejoinder. "But we don't want to. Smoking is a lot of fun, and you will miss it."

"The reason I don't believe you when you say that you could quit if you wanted to is that I fooled myself that way. I told myself I was just playing around with the stuff—then my mother asked me to quit. Well, it was a challenge to my will power, and I told her I'd quit. I thought it would be a snap, but all I ask is for you to endure what I have endured—then have someone poke it under your nose and you will see what it takes to say No."

John turned away, and the fellows did not tempt him again, for it became noised about that his mother was pretty sick, and there was a question as to whether she would get well. One of the fellows in the crowd actually decided to quit, and did, though he had a harder time even than John. He had smoked longer, and he had to go home each day to a house full of smoke, for his father was a smoker. That made it almost unbearable.

John took to sitting with his mother a little while each evening, and she talked to him of things he had not dreamed of before. When she disclosed the fact that she had dedicated him to the ministry, he was dismayed.

*J*OHN NOW TOOK to sitting with his mother a little while each evening, and she talked to him of things he had not dreamed of before. One evening she told him that she had dedicated him to be a minister when he was only a small babe.

John was aghast!

"A *minister*, Mother!" he exclaimed, hardly able to credit his ears. She began then to tell him a little of herself, and the life she and Emil had had in the years before he was born. He knew not the smallest iota of their former hopes, joys, and aspirations. He had hardly heard of Battle Creek. Jeanie had him climb up to the top closet shelf and get the old picture brochures. She showed him her picture in her long nurse's dress with a tiny, high-fluted cap that trained nurses wore then. There was a picture of Emil, too, in a fine broadcloth suit, taken in a studio in Battle Creek. John gazed at all of them with interest.

Even Jeanie did not know that Battle Creek College had been moved to Berrien Springs, Michigan, and the American Medical College had closed its doors forever. John had not known these places existed, much less had loomed so large in the lives of his father and mother.

"And when we came here your father gave up all hope of being a doctor—but we were not here on the

123

farm a year before we realized we had made a mistake. Grandma always grieved because we came back. Then when you were born, it seemed to father and me that in you we might realize the hopes we both had of doing great things for the Lord."

"But Mother," John had protested, "I want to go into some kind of business. I feel like I am—well, fitted for that kind of thing. I would not know the first thing about being a minister, and—well, I want to take a business course. I'd like to go to the university next winter, for if I can stay at Uncle Sterns's I can get through in a couple of years."

Jeanie turned her face to the wall, and John tried to cheer her up. She was so thin and pale that he thought about her all the next day. And poor dad, too. He was like a ship without a rudder. He needed mother and her advice more than he cared to admit. Things never went as well in the business when she was not around, and the nurse and the doctor took a huge bite out of the income, and that was an uncomfortable fact. Emil might bicker and argue with Jeanie, but nevertheless he needed her, and nothing seemed to go well without her.

To everyone's relief Jeanie began to mend and was soon up and around. The nurse was dismissed and Trudie Haden, one of the neighbor girls, did most of the heavy work. When Jeanie took over again, things began to run smoothly. Dad began to look brighter and to bring his problems home to Jeanie. Things began to prosper, as of old, and John entered the new semester with high hopes and great zest. He went over to Oak City and enrolled in some university classes in business, making himself at home in a big room in Uncle Sterns's ample upstairs. He planned on being back on the farm every weekend. His mind buzzed with the delight of the new life he was planning for himself. Business spelling, shorthand, bookkeeping, accounting, typing—how eagerly he conned the list of courses.

He took some of the money he had saved and bought one of the best typewriters he could find. Uncle Sterns gave him an old roll-top desk that had been replaced with one more modern. John set up his room into a sort of compact little office and made up his mind that he was going to get all he could out of his classes and not fool around like some of the other fellows did. This was his big chance to make good, and he made up his mind to do it.

ONE DAY—HE would remember that day as long as he lived—he was in bookkeeping class, and they were making out bills and receipts. The professor had just called on him to go to the board when a knock at the door called him out of the room. It was Uncle Sterns. His kind old eyes were clouded with sympathy.

"Look here, John, you had better get your hat and books and come home with me. It's your mom. She has taken bad again, and they have gone out to the house to get her ready to go to the hospital. And from what Emil said she ain't going to make it, for the doctor says there ain't a chance in a hundred she'll live."

John stood looking at Uncle Sterns, hardly able to credit his ears with what he heard. Why, when he left home only Monday mom was out in the yard with scissors and was cutting a bouquet for the dining table. He had waved at her, and she had waved the whole big bouquet back at him and had smiled so sweetly as he went away.

"Not going to make it?" he repeated, hardly grasping what his kind old uncle had said.

"No, that's what your pa said. And it must be so, for he broke down tellin' me about it. He said for you to hurry. Doc said she might live a day or a week, and she might go today. Come on, John." And the old man led the way out of the wide polished hall.

John got his books, his coat, and his hat. They stopped briefly for him to pack his grip and they were flying in his uncle's Model-T over the dusty roads toward home. He tried to imagine what life was going to be like without his mother. She was the hub of the family. What would life be like; what would they all do without her?

What would happen to May Rachel and to Fritz and

to little Fred, who was only a year old? John knew that if mother died, he would have to quit school and take hold of things and help to run the home and take care of the younger children. Dad was all right in the barn and on the farm, but in the house he was helpless. He could not do a thing, for grandpa and grandma both had had the idea that doing housework was feminine, and not a man's work at all. It had been a source of a lot of trouble between mother and father too, for when mother had spent all day out with the men, helping to do the bookkeeping at the office they had set up in the barn, she could not understand why dad could not take hold and help her a little. It made for a lot of bitterness, and John had secretly sided with his mother. What was sauce for the goose ought to be sauce for the gander.

THE FORD TURNED in at the familiar driveway of the lovely house that dad had built as a monument to his pride. On a great knoll of land, it stood with evergreens grouped all around it. A huge, circular screened-in porch dominated one corner, and a tower room embellished the other. But over it hung a pall of sadness, or so it seemed to John as he took his bag from the back seat and hastened to the door. Little Fred toddled to meet him, and John saw he needed someone to see to him. His rompers were a sight and his face was dirty. Trudie was not the manager that mother was. He called Trudie and turned the baby over to her before he went upstairs.

He stood at the door of his mother's room and wiped his eyes before he could enter. His father came out of a bedroom down the hall in time to see his boy before he went in to see his mother. Silently he drew John into the bedroom across the hall and closed the door.

When John turned to face his father he was shocked to see the change that a few weeks had made in him. He had no idea that his mother's illness had been so devastating to his father's health. He was a broken man, a mere shadow of what he had been. The ominous illness, and all it portended, seemed to have taken the spirit out of him.

"She isn't going to live, John," he whispered huskily, his breath catching in little gasps and convulsions that shook his big frame. It was as if the very thought of life without his Jeanie would be the death of him too.

He was weeping now, great shuddering sobs, and he clung to John with such a grasp that his fingers bit into his son's arm. He covered his eyes with a large blue handkerchief, and John put his arm around his father's heaving shoulders.

"She hasn't got a chance, John, the doctor said," he told his son, his voice broken and sad. "And I haven't been good to her, I haven't; and now it is too late. I can't make it up to her for the coldness, the blame, the mean and hateful words I've had for her—and her so capable and so good."

"Don't, Dad," John sobbed, feeling as if he could not stand it. "Mother loved you, and I think she must have known you didn't mean some of the things you said—I think she must have, Dad."

John had heard some of the shouted words in the years gone by, so he had small comfort to offer.

"Your mother was an unusual woman, John, and there will never be another like her. And I did worse than be mean to her, son. I led her away from God. I took her away from the work God laid out for her to do. I was the one who began to leave off having God first and foremost in the home—she didn't follow for years."

The two clung to each other in the throes of their grief, neither knowing what more to say to assuage the grief of the other. Finally John went to the bathroom and washed his face in cold water.

"I've got to see her, Dad," John said. He went across the hall and stepped into the room. She was sleeping, so lightly, so quietly, that it seemed as if she did not breathe. John stood looking down at her and thought of how lovely she must have been when she was young, for even now she was lovely. Her fine features seemed as though carved out of marble. Her hair swept back from her forehead and had not even a streak of gray in it. John thought, looking down at her, how terrible it would be to have a home without mother—so sweet, so tender, and so capable. Then she opened her eyes, and a look of pleasure flitted into them at the sight of her big boy. He stooped and kissed her. She put up her thin hand and rumpled his hair. The doctor had decided against an operation, for as he told father, it would do no good, so why add suffering to what was inevitable?

SHE LIVED ONLY a week. She was so sweet and so loving that the whole household seemed to go to the sickroom to borrow courage for the day ahead. John never saw a time like it.

It did something to old grandpa, too. After she was laid out in the beautiful velvet casket, and it was placed in the living room, as things used to be done in the olden days, the old man went in many times a day to see her before the funeral. He seemed like a different person. He had never been friendly to anyone, and now it was as though he was the chief mourner instead of Emil and the children.

He was sitting in the kitchen by the table after supper on the day before the funeral, looking so disconsolate that John felt sorry for him and pulled up a chair and sat with him.

He was moved to tell him that he did not think he could resume his education now that mother was gone, though why he should have mentioned it to grandpa he could not explain. Everyone knew that the old man was dead against education beyond what a person needed to sign his name to a note, or figure up bushels and acres.

"Your mother'd want ye to go on, Johnny," the old man had said, surprisingly enough. "And I fer one think ye ort to, for Jeanie was right in most things—more right than your pa. And she had a good business head, too, and helped Emil to get ahead."

They sat there in silence for a little while, then the old man turned and said in a whisper to the boy: "Did she ever tell you anything about Battle Creek, and her bein' a fine nurse there, Johnny?"

"Not much, Grandpa. What about it?"

"I've heard ma and Emil both say she was one of the best, so that Dr. Kellogg himself once gave it out that she was a fine example of what a real Christian nurse ought to be. She was a Seventh-day Adventist, and so was your father too, for that matter, and your Uncle Ernest as well, though he hasn't been faithful to it any more than Emil has."

John looked at the old man incredulously.

"A Seventh-day Adventist," he repeated. "Do you mean they kept Saturday like—like——"

The old man laughed harshly.

131

"Like I have?" he asked, his tired old eyes seeking John's. "No, John, no, no, no. I have known the right— yes, I have known it. But the devil himself had no one who fought truth more than I have. I often wondered how grandma put up with me, I have led such a sorry, mean life. No, your ma, she was a lady, and she walked in real beauty, like I heard someone say oncet. She kept Saturday like God wanted folks to keep it, from love in the heart and from a real gladness to do what was right. No, John, not like I did, no, never."

"You mean, Grandpa, that Saturday *is* the right day to keep, and we have not been doing it?"

"There ain't no question about it."

"And dad knows this?"

"He knows it like the back of his hand, but he don't know I know. He ain't had a happy day since he left off doing right, and he don't know I know that, either."

"Grandpa, do you know mother's sister, Aunt Mary?"

"Her as is a nurse down in the South? Oh, yes; I have seen her a time or two. She appeared to be a real good woman. All the Adventists are, far as I can see."

"She sent us papers for a while. We children surely liked them—was she an Adventist too?"

"Sure, sure, John, and still is, far as I know. She never fell away like your ma and pa did."

"Grandpa, whatever got into mother and father to make them change?"

132

"Oh, they got the money-making bee in their bonnets. Ma always argued that I hadn't ought to have urged Emil to come home. He was fixin' t' take the medical course, and I told 'm they could have this place if they came home.

"But I know now I hadn't ought to have done it, and it has plagued me a lot, for they ain't made much in doin' it, not nothing like they ought to have made, for they have had an awful lot of bad luck, and where they made a lot of money they have lost a lot, too. I've got eyes; I can see."

JOHN SAT for a long time and thought of what grandpa had said. He had never seen the old man so subdued. Usually he was so abrupt and harsh that he had never been a favorite with the grandchildren, but John put his arm awkwardly across the old man's stooped shoulders before he shuffled off to bed, for he had stayed here with Emil and Jeanie since ma had died. Grandpa had given John a new vista of the life of his parents he had never even suspected. So his parents had been Adventists, and dad almost had taken the medical course. He had to put all of these thoughts away, for the funeral and the subsequent adjustments were all so painful he hardly had time to call his own. The whole household was like a rudderless ship, with Jeanie gone.

John had brought back his things from the university

and had set the new typewriter, the new clothes, the reams of paper, and the hardly used textbooks in his room, but he had no time to use any of them, for he had more than he could do in the days that followed. He wondered how mother ever did all she did. Now they could not seem to keep a hired girl. They quit almost as fast as they were hired, for there was no system about anything. Finally John essayed to take over the management of the house. Clumsy though he was, he was faced with being a nurse-maid, a cook, a baker, a housekeeper, and a seamstress.

During the next three months John did everything from washing baby Fred's small garments to putting up a batch of pickles from the garden and patching dad's overalls on mother's sewing machine. But he was ready to tear out his hair. Where was life leading him? It was not that he did not want to do his part in what was an emergency of the first magnitude, but he knew he was not doing a good job of it, and it could not continue. He could not bake bread as it should be. He could not mend the clothes neatly. Something had gone radically wrong with the working machinery of the whole household. He did not get one end of the house cleaned up before other parts were in shambles. It was maddening. It reminded him of what his grandmother had once said when something she was doing seemed to lick her. "I am like the old woman who tried to mop up the sea," she had said.

John felt like that old woman. As he contemplated his

situation, he could not understand how his mother had kept up with so much work, for even though she had a hired girl some of the time, John knew that she had spent many hours on dad's work and on the books, and she had done a lot of things for people in town, too. She had sent out the statements to the milk customers and balanced all the books at the end of the month. She did a thousand things he did not even consider doing, such as canning, and drying the fruits and vegetables, and making and mending the clothes. He realized then how much he had added to his mother's burdens by his bickering with the younger children and throwing his things around and not picking up and doing for himself as he should have done.

But what of his own life? What of his own future? Must he stay forever and be scrubbing potatoes, carrying out ashes, and watching little Fred? Would life deal him such a blow as this and make it impossible, and even dishonorable, to pursue his own burning ambitions? Father did not seem to realize *he* had a life. He did not seem to see that time was passing and his son was not in any way preparing for the life he had chosen for himself.

John always thought it was grandpa who had solved the problem for him, for he told him one day in the kitchen that he hoped he would not let his life go to waste as his father had done, even though the old man himself took the blame.

"But what am I to do?" John queried, almost petulantly. "I have to take care of things here, for who would do it if I didn't? May Rachel and Fritz couldn't, even if they didn't go to school."

"There's a way, even if you can't see it," the old man answered. "If grandma had lived and had her health she'd have been glad to come in and do for the children; but— you will think me funny to say this—but your mother would have said to pray about it, if it was in the days when she first came here. She had a lot of faith in prayin'. 'Twouldn't do no harm t' try. I couldn't tell you how, but there is a way."

JOHN THOUGHT a lot about what his grandfather had said that evening, and he thought of his grandmother, too. He had loved her so, and she had loved him as one of her own. She had talked and confided in him, too, and urged him to make something of his life. He never forgot.

Once she had told him she had never in her life got to do anything she wanted to do. John had been curious at that. Grandma had seemed so sad, so detached, she had hardly seemed like a person to him; more like a well-oiled piece of machinery that turned out work silently. She was especially so when grandpa was around.

"In Germany I learned to read all by myself," she

had told him. "My brothers were allowed to go to school, but not us girls. I used to go and get their books when I was making up the beds, and I learned. I did not dare to tell, for my parents thought it was needless for a girl to learn—it might make her proud. I thought, Johnny, if we came to the New World, Hans and I, we might get a chance, someway, somehow—I thought I might teach school. I might write a book. Oh, I could tell such wondrous things of the olden days in Germany—but I never got to."

"You did not get to do things you liked, Grandma?" John's heart was melting with pity.

"When I saw I could not do that, I thought to dress up the girls and make the house pretty as I often dreamed —but there never was a chance. I wanted to read in books, too, but well, Hans never liked it, and what reading I did was done in secret; and it is hard to have dreams and not be able to share them. So I guess I have lived a pretty useless life."

John thought of all this after grandpa had gone to bed. It would not be long, he pondered, till old Hans would be gone too, to lie beside old grandma who had dreamed such bright and hopeless dreams. And mother was sleeping out there now too, her dreams unrealized. What was life, anyway? Would nothing endure? Would mother and father and grandpa and grandma all serve this black soil and die, and that be the end? Was that life? John thought long and earnestly on the matter.

What bright hopes mother and father had had, so he pondered, only to have them all go to nothing, with mother gone so young. He thought, too, of the religion they had given up, and he remembered how mother had grieved over that. It had seemed to him so unnecessary, for mother was good, and dear, and had always been so.

So the days passed by. John worked hard, but things piled up so much that he wondered how it would end. He could not keep it up, for he just did not know how, and his heart was not in it.

ONE DAY a letter came from Aunt Mary, who had not been able to attend the funeral because of an accident. She was at a sanitarium in Madison, Tennessee. John remembered the interest she had taken in them all through the years, and her letter was welcome, for she asked in great detail what they were doing and how they were getting along. The tone of the letter led John to believe that Aunt Mary could come and take over if she were asked to do so. His heart gave a great leap. If he were only released from this hateful housework he could go on and finish his commercial course or maybe he could study law, or politics, or even teaching methods. When father came in for supper he looked so sad and tired that John realized that he too needed the domestic side of his life settled if he was to avoid breaking under the strain.

While John took up supper and filled little Freddie's bottle, they all sat down to eat. John handed Aunt Mary's letter to his father to read. He noted as he read it that his face relaxed, as if some weighty problem was rolled from his shoulders.

"I believe she'd come, John, and sure enough, we need her. You're doin' all you can, but you ought to be in school, and don't think I don't know it. Want to write and ask her to come, son?"

"I surely will, Dad," John answered. "I will write that letter tonight—soon as I get things cleared up and get the baby off to bed."

"You write it, and I will see what I can do to the dishes," he said looking around a little helplessly. "You hadn't ought to carry all this load."

For answer, Aunt Mary came without announcement, bag and baggage, and telephoned Emil to meet her. John observed that his father was almost gay as he got the car out to go to the station. To tell the truth, Emil was so relieved he hardly knew what to do. Nothing had gone right since his Jeanie had gone. Maybe Mary would straighten things out and give him a little peace of mind. That her religion might wake up the watchdogs of his sleeping conscience, he had not even considered. The old Battle Creek days, when he was truly enjoying the religion he had chosen, seemed to belong to another life, and he hardly ever thought of it any more. He sensed that Jeanie had been under conviction the last few months of her life and had tried to set her spiritual house in order. She had tried to talk to him a time or two, but they had grown apart so much that he resented even her gentle observations and was harsh with her. After that she did not say much any more, only to remark that she had feared they had committed the unpardonable sin. He had worried about that for quite a while, but when she let the subject drop, he settled back into his old ways.

On the way out from town Aunt Mary had told Emil the conditions on which she would stay. Emil thought to himself that she had him at a disadvantage, and he could not do much else but agree. She must be free to have worship with the children, and she would not have a thing to do with meat of any kind or with coffee or tea. He knew they were not good, and if she was to do the cooking she was not going to have to use them. And John was to be allowed to go on to school. In his heart, Emil knew all these things were right, and he vaguely wondered how in the world he and Jeanie had wandered so far afield, doing the things they knew very well were wrong. Yet, because Mary had caught them transgressing so flagrantly, he was a little nettled at her taking undue advantage the way she did. It was a mingling of pride and shame, to be sure, but Emil felt ruffled just the same.

But he was so glad to see her and to have her take over that he said not a word, but let her have her way. He carried her bags in and had John come and help with the trunk. They put her in Jeanie's room, because it was cheerful and pleasant, and it seemed right for it to be occupied. It was near to the heart of things, too, and it was good to have the shades rolled up and the door open again.

$\mathcal{A}$ UNT MARY WAS a woman of about forty, her pretty light-brown hair fluffing about her slim face. She had brown eyes and a firm determined mouth, but there was about her whole demeanor something very much like mother, and yet a little more decided and determined than mother had been. She washed her face and hands in the bathroom and donned a neat blue-print dress, then hurried down to the kitchen. John went in to help her, and she shooed him out.

"Now, you just run along, Johnny," she said kindly. "I think you have done your stint, and I mean to have you back in school before we can say Jack Robinson. I have a feeling you can catch up, even though you have been out some time. You look as though you have it in you."

John turned to go, but she called him back.

"I may need you to run into the village to get some things, for it looks to me as though your supplies are away down," she said. "But you go up and get your clothes in order, and bring down the things to be washed or mended. I will get to them as fast as I can."

She was up on a small stepladder, taking things out of the cupboards. The whole kitchen was in such a "mare's nest," John wondered how anyone could ever get things straightened up. When he came down later, she had emptied all of one cupboard and had put some white shelf paper on the scrubbed shelves. In an hour she had done more organizing than he had done since mother died. It just seemed as though all he could do was to poke things into a cupboard, wherever they would fit in, whether they belonged there or not. And such a mess!

There were several packages of baking powder, all partly used. Jars of peanut butter, some full and some partly used, vied for space with a half-dozen jars of jelly. There was flour in a bowl and flour in a pie pan that had been used to dip something in for frying. Stale bread, stale cake, and a dried-up piece of pie, which no one remembered having left on the shelf, were put into a pail for the chickens.

"You needed me all right," Aunt Mary said grimly, smelling a fruit jar that contained a sticky something with a moldy odor. "By the way, John, you get all the meat and the pork out of the icebox and throw it out. And throw this out too," she said, handing him a pail of lard. "I won't have the stuff around. You just ought to hear the way Dr. Kellogg talked about hogs and lard. You wouldn't be able to stomach it, if you did."

Emil came in during the process, and though he smiled a little dubiously, he said not a word.

WHEN JOHN GATHERED up the things that Aunt Mary had told him to throw out, he demurred a little and told her it seemed a shame to destroy so much good food.

"Good food!" Aunt Mary had exclaimed a little testily. "To think I would see any home—any *one*, I mean —who ever knew what it meant to be a real Adventist, and a Battle Creek Adventist at that, with *lard* in the kitchen. Listen here, John, it is impossible for a creature like a hog to be healthy, for you know as well as I know that they feed on every detestable thing. There is nothing a dirty old hog won't eat—and their flesh is made up from the corruption they take into their bodies. We are what we eat, don't you know that, John?"

143

John turned away in loathing, for he remembered only the week before when Cy, the farm hand, had killed a big rattlesnake. He impaled it on the tine of his hay fork and threw it over to the hogs. They made short work of it, and it made him so sick that he had to turn away.

"Dr. Kellogg used to tell us when he talked to us nurses that swine's flesh of *all* flesh produces a bad state of the blood, and I won't have the stuff around, I tell you."

When John came in from throwing out the huge pile of what she termed rubbish, he saw she had made at least a start on the kitchen, and she was preparing supper. She had some cans of something on the table she had brought down from upstairs. John picked one can up. "Protose," he read. It was made by the Battle Creek Food Company. Aunt Mary glanced at him.

"That is a nut meat, and I remember that Emil used to love it the way I fixed it when I visited Jeanie in Battle Creek once, and we had him over to dinner. It has no disease germs or uric acid and stale decaying blood, thank you, but real life-giving elements to help a person to be really well. I am going to fix some the way your mother and I used to fix it."

John had cooked so long for the little family that he was curious about the things that appeared on the table that night. They were delicious beyond belief, and Emil ate as though starved. The graham gems had been baked in the iron gem pans that Emil said Jeanie had brought from Battle Creek, and which had gone through the fire that burned their house down. Mary explained that they had no baking powder in them, but that the batter was raised by beating iced milk and graham flour till it was full of air bubbles, after which it had been put into hot iron pans and baked in the oven. The protose had been scalloped with celery, onions, and tomatoes, and baked till it was crusty and delicious. A head of cabbage had been shredded and mixed with cottage cheese that she had taken the time to make from some clabbered milk she found; this had been dressed with a homemade dressing made by mixing cream with lemon, honey, and a little salt. Potatoes from their field had been roasted and heaped up in a platter ready for the Savita gravy she had made. The dessert was rice pudding filled with plump raisins, shredded pineapple, and black walnuts. How she had gotten ready such a feast was a marvel to John, who had struggled over the plainest of fare, only to have one thing scorch while he was stirring and attending to another. It was unbelievable.

John helped Aunt Mary do the dishes; in fact, he did them while she cleaned out the dish cupboard. When he offered to do them she said, "Well, honey, I tell you, I will let you do that, for I don't want to wait till morning to get this cupboard in shape." Then she showed John how to sort the dishes and to clean them off a little before plumping them into the dishwater. "Get all the glass tumblers and the silver into piles, honey," she told him. "Wash them first. There is a right and a wrong way of doing everything, even dishes."

She cleaned out the big ice refrigerator, and Emil brought in a hundred-pound block of ice that day. She showed John how to cover everything before he put it away, so it would not taste like the icebox. Then she flew at the cupboard with all the vim she had, and did not seem a bit tired. It was so pleasant, working beside this sweet, voluble woman who seemed to be able to give a reason for all the things she did. John noticed with pleasure how she organized things, so different from the hired girls they had employed. Most of them did their work in a slap-dash fashion and were gone the minute the dishcloth was thrown on a nail and the dishpan inverted on the sink.

"Now, back to that pork business, John," she said as she sorted saucers and slipped some dirty ones into the sink for him to wash. "It is horrible, and I believe if we knew all the reasons the good Lord had for prohibiting men to use it, we would have the secret as to why there are so many terrible diseases like cancer, tuberculosis, and heart trouble."

"Do you honestly believe that, Aunt Mary?" John asked. "Is it really set down in the Bible that man ought not to eat pork and lard and things like that?"

$\mathscr{A}$UNT MARY STOPPED her work long enough to regard the lad with astonishment.

"To think that Jeanie and Emil should rear you in such ignorance of the real vital and living things of life. Why, John, they knew these things like the backs of their own hands," she exclaimed. "I don't know what got into my sister, or into your father either, John," she said, coming over to where he stood by the sink, his hands immersed in the soapy water. She laid a firm hand on his shoulders.

"John," she repeated. "You and I have to get this household in order. We have got to restore the old paths. I mean get the whole household back to where the Lord can pour out His blessing. You know, John, the Bible says that he that knoweth to do good and doeth it not, to him it is sin, and it also says, 'Your iniquities have separated between you and your God, and your sins have hid his face from you, that he will not hear.' No wonder things have not gone right. You have not had the Lord's blessing."

John pondered that.

"You said something about restoring old paths, Aunt Mary; I don't get that. What do you mean by that?" Aunt Mary turned and looked at John as her swift fingers were turning the chaos of the cupboard into perfect order.

"That's Bible too, John, and it goes something like this—oh, but wait a moment and I will read it to you. I

147

can't quote it exactly, and I want you to enjoy the beauty of the text as it is written."

She had planned this discussion with John to the finest detail, and from her capacious apron pocket she brought out a small copy of the Bible. She leafed through it rapidly and surely. John could only admire the way she did even the reading of the Bible, for as with everything else, she wanted it to be exact.

"Here it is in Isaiah 58:12," she said eagerly, in the same tone she would have used if she had found a rare treasure. " 'And they that shall be of thee shall build the old waste places: thou shalt raise up the foundations of many generations; and thou shalt be called, The repairer of the breach, The restorer of paths to dwell in.' "

"I don't see how in the world you can take a text like that and make any sense out of it," John said slowly, feeling that he must be honest with the good and dear little lady. He began to have a secret conviction that she was a little bit fanatical, and it disappointed him a little.

"That is one of the easiest texts in the Bible to understand, John. I don't have to stretch my imagination a bit to explain that to you. It nearly tears me up to think that Jeanie's boy would not know these things like the ABC's. The same prophet who spoke this, Isaiah, said, 'Bind up the testimony, seal the law among my disciples.' And John, the seal of God's holy law is found right in the heart of the law—in the fourth commandment. You know what a seal is. It's the mark on any official document that makes it official—a sign of authority that presents the credentials of the person who is setting forth its legality, to show it is not a fraud."

"I get that," John agreed. "I know what a seal is. We get stuff notarized and it isn't worth a thing if the seal isn't there. It wouldn't be accepted."

"You see, the fourth, or the Sabbath, commandment gives all the things required to make a document official, and without it the whole Decalogue could be called fraudulent. Removing or changing the seal makes a document of no value, and of course, as far as the Ten Commandments are concerned, that is where the enemy went to work."

"That's clear," John put in, watching her animated face with new interest.

"Well, John, although the Papacy substituted the Sunday rest day in the place of the Sabbath of the Lord, this text exhorts the disciples of the Lord to restore it and to return the Sabbath of the fourth commandment to its rightful position as the Creator's memorial of creation."

"Then *that* is the breach spoken of in the verse?"

"Of course. It is a break right in the heart of the Ten Commandments, and intended to be a death blow. We must repair that breach in this home, and the next verses, Isaiah 58:13 and 14, can be a glorious promise we can all claim. I know it by heart, but you read it, John."

John took the tiny Bible and read the text Aunt Mary indicated.

" 'If thou turn away thy foot from the sabbath, from doing thy pleasure on my holy day; and call the sabbath a delight, the holy of the Lord, honourable; and shalt honour him, not doing thine own ways, nor finding thine own pleasure, nor speaking thine own words: then shalt thou delight thyself in the Lord; and I will cause thee to ride upon the high places of the earth, and feed thee with the heritage of Jacob thy father: for the mouth of the Lord hath spoken it.' "

"You see, John," Aunt Mary went on, "it is curious, but the Sabbath commandment is the only one that the Lord told us to 'remember,' and it is the one that the whole world has forgotten. In order to restore the foundations of many generations, we need to make worship of God and love for Him first and foremost in our lives. As the patriarchs did, we need to erect an altar to Him wherever we pitch our tent."

"How do you mean—'erect an altar,' and 'pitch our tent'? All those terms are Greek to me, Auntie."

"I keep forgetting, John. They were almost household words with us, but it means to set out to worship God in the way He wants us to worship Him. Some folks say we should worship Him this way and others say that way, but we should study to worship Him in *His* way and make consideration of God the first thing in our lives."

"This Saturday Sabbath business—I guess I have sort of turned against it because of the way grandpa used to keep Saturday. I never heard of anyone doing it that way, and it didn't seem good to me; and I think it discouraged mother too, but I can't say for sure."

"We must not be led astray by the mistakes of anyone, John, though I think your grandpa has mellowed a lot from what he used to be. From what I have read, that is the way the Pharisees and the Sadducees did. They made of the Sabbath a burden, and not a delight, until the people were ready for the paganism that Satan had ready for them. Keeping the Sabbath should be such a delight to us that we shall long for its coming each week and see its closing with regret."

WHAT DOES ALL THIS have to do with lard and pork, Auntie? I can see that you may have something on the matter of the Sabbath, though I would like to study it a little on my own, but what does God care whether it is a pork chop or a lamb chop, a piece of sausage or a piece of that canned meat substitute you brought? With millions of homes and millions of people, and perhaps billions of worlds to be concerned with, how can God care about such a trivial thing?"

"It isn't trivial, John. It is of great consequence, because you are of great importance to Him. You cannot be healthy and eat vile things that feed on the filth of the earth. You are what you eat. What you eat, John, determines whether you will have good or bad blood coursing in your veins. I had this thing impressed on me year after year in Battle Creek, and in every class I attended."

"Battle Creek must have been a wonderful place," observed John. "Mother spoke of it so glowingly, when she spoke of it at all. I noticed another thing, too, since we are talking of it. Mother did not work on Saturday for a good many months before she died. Now I am glad that she didn't, if she believed it as you do. Come to think of it, I don't believe she ate any pork either."

"Well, it is no good," Aunt Mary said vehemently. "It is impossible for it to be anything but diseased when hogs feed on the detestable things the way they do. It stands to reason that if human beings feed on their flesh, they are corrupted by the same impurities. One author wrote, and I read it myself, that pork eating causes intense suffering to the human race. And that's not all to consider, either, for Isaiah 66 says that those who are eating swine's flesh will be consumed. I am not going to stop lifting my voice against its use."

Aunt Mary and John had by this time gotten the kitchen in apple-pie order, and she kissed him good night and told him to go to bed, so he could get up early enough to see about getting back to school. So ended the first day of Aunt Mary's stay with the Huener family. John went to bed to ponder what she had told him, and he determined to search out the real truth for himself. He was not quite convinced, and he wanted to make sure before he burned any bridges behind him.

The next morning, when Emil went into town with a load of corn, John went with him and took the train to Capital City to see about entering school. In the hope that he would be accepted, he took a suitcase full of necessities. He would stay if he could and come back and get the rest of his things on a weekend.

WHILE JOHN WAS AWAY at the business college, taking up where he left off, Aunt Mary was at work on the ones who were left behind. May Rachel and Fritz and little Freddie took to her enthusiastically, and the machinery of the big household began to run as smooth as clockwork. Emil paid Aunt Mary a wage and told her she could add to it by selling eggs and cottage cheese and butter if she was a mind to; and she was, for she had big plans in mind for the children.

Grandpa died that winter, and Emil had a bad case of quinsy. Aunt Mary took care of him efficiently with hot packs, or fomentations, and she dosed the grumbling man with more herbs and fruit juices than he had had for years. He could not help admitting that he got well in a hurry, and even the family doctor was enthusiastic and asked Aunt Mary whether she would go on "cases" occasionally. He told her he would like to work with a nurse like her.

One weekend when John was home he was pleased with the way things were being taken care of. May Rachel looked so pretty in the dresses Aunt Mary had made for her out of material mother had in a big trunk in the attic. Fritz was doing much better in school, and he had taken over the care of the chickens. Aunt Mary was sharing the egg money with him, and he was proudly showing everyone his bankbook. He had saved $37.05 already, and that was good for a thirteen-year-old boy. Aunt Mary told Emil that this was the best way to teach a boy responsibility and initiative and said that before long she was going to urge him to buy his own clothes.

John had let his mind slip about the Sabbath though, forgetting that it began at sundown on Friday night. The house was spotless when he came in, and the kitchen was a place of real beauty. Aunt Mary had made whole-wheat bread and the fat loaves had been oiled and placed on a snowy linen towel to cool. There was a shelf of cinnamon rolls bulging with nuts and raisins and lacquered with a honeyed syrup, rich and buttery. A big earthen bowl of beans, baked with tomato and onion and crusty on top, made John wish it was suppertime already. And there was a meatless meat loaf. Aunt Mary told him proudly that it was made of bread crumbs, rice, lentils, onions, celery, and a can of nut roast. It looked and smelled savory and delicious, even though John was wary of concoctions. He saw that she had brewed some cereal coffee, and he sensed that dad's habit of guzzling coffee every time he came into the house was being put into abeyance, for even he admitted that it was not in the least good for him and made him jittery and sleepless. The sun was not yet down when they all sat down to the table in the clean dining room and ate cinnamon rolls, potato soup, and whole-wheat toast croutons (as Aunt Mary called little squares of buttered toast) crisped in the oven. The dessert was a big wedge of cherry pie.

John noted that May Rachel looked very neat in a dress that was starched and suitable, and Fritz and little Fred looked cared for and happy. Even dad changed his clothes before supper, a thing unheard of since John could remember.

May Rachel and Aunt Mary straightened up the dishes, and Fritz got little Freddie into his nightie, as if he had done it all his life. They then gathered in the living room, and Aunt Mary got a book. They all gathered around her. John was amused to notice that even Emil, his father, had hitched his chair near enough to hear when she read to the children, his face wistful with memories of days that were no more.

It was a pretty sight. Little Freddie sat on her lap, his thumb in his little mouth, and Fritz and May were on footstools in front of her. The book she was reading was a book of short stories. Its title was *Sabbath Readings for the Home Circle*. The story she read tonight was about a man who early in life had learned to cheat and lie. It told of how it finally got him into the penitentiary. He had learned as a child to deceive, and in the courtroom he cursed his mother for not teaching him to do right, so that he might have been saved from the frightful experience of going to prison. When Aunt Mary got through with the story they begged for another one, and she read them one more; but they had their prayers right there at Auntie's knee before they went to bed. John was a little puzzled, but he was glad on the whole and pleased with things as they were going. It made him resolve to go on to college.

TWO YEARS WENT BY. John had not done anything about what Auntie had told him, and he tried to forget it and to tell himself that it was not of great importance. The more he disregarded what he really knew was sound and right, the more prejudiced he became toward Aunt Mary and her influence over May Rachel and Fritz. They were bigger now—May was fifteen and Fritz was thirteen. They were openly and unashamedly keeping the Sabbath, and they were going in the buggy with Aunt Mary to a town some twelve miles away to church. But now Aunt Mary had another bee in her bonnet, so Emil wrote to his son in one of his rare letters.

"John," he wrote, "I get plain disgusted with Aunt Mary, for she is going to great lengths here at the house, and sometimes I am sorry that I sent for her. She has the children all in a flurry to attend a camp meeting. There is no need for that, as you well know. We got along without such things for a good many years, and now all May and Fritz talk about is camp meeting, camp meeting, camp meeting. I never saw the like of it. Seems like a fellow can't ever have a bit of peace. But don't say a word in a letter about this, son, for I don't want Mary to get mad and quit on us. We could do worse, I suppose, but I do get tired of her trying to convert us all the time."

John could see the injustice of his father's attitude, and he knew that his father had hardly paid his sister-in-law a thing for her two years of hard work. He owed her a lot for the frugality and the economy she exercised in the care of the huge household. He knew he would be hard put to get anyone who would even do a tithe of what she did. He only felt piqued at her because she was a living rebuke to him. He was not living right and he well knew it.

Aunt Mary had discovered a whole trunkful of dress goods that Jeanie had stored away. She went to work making a lot of pretty ruffly dresses for May Rachel, and some neat shirts for Fritz, and little suits for Freddie. They were all to be fitted out for camp meeting in fine shape.

Thus it was that Emil did not have to put up any money for the fine camp meeting vacation that filled all their talk. He had primed himself to refuse highhandedly if they asked him for money to outfit themselves, but he was ashamed of himself when he found that Mary had found time to make for him a half dozen fine shirts and had them folded and put in his dresser drawer. She dulled the very shafts he had aimed to use against her. When he tried to bluster a little and to ask who in the world would do the work while she and the children were gone for ten days, she had the answer ready for him.

"Oh, Emil, I have already asked Celia Barton, and she is coming in the morning for me to tell her how to do things, and you know she is good and dependable. You pay her fifteen dollars for the ten days. I arranged that so you would not have to bother."

He almost snarled in reply, but not quite. Aunt Mary had a sense of humor and smiled to herself after he had gone, for his grouches did not worry her a bit. She knew he was fighting his conscience, and she renewed her diligence in praying for him and for John.

Elias, the hired man, took them to the train the day they left, and they were on their way with light hearts and great anticipation. To Auntie it was an old story, and she had all the makings of a tent home in her big trunk. She had curtains to divide it in the middle, as well as sheets, pillows, and bedding. She had put in three hot-water bottles, and a little kerosene stove was boxed up and shipped. A few dishes and some cutlery and a pan or two were put in.

"Some of the nights get cold," Aunt Mary explained to May. "The hot-water bottles will come in handy; you will see. And you will get ravenously hungry sleeping outdoors like that."

"Where will we eat, Aunt Mary?" asked Fritz, who was always interested in food.

"We will keep breakfast food in our tent, and we can buy milk," she had said practically. "And besides, you can go to the kitchen and buy good cooked cereal. We can eat breakfast in our tent. I know a place near the campground where they sell wonderful fruit. We can have all the apples, pears, and peaches that we can eat. We will eat dinner and supper in the dining hall. I want you to taste the wonderful meatless roasts they make, and when we get time we will try all of them out in the kitchen, May."

So away they went. John heard only echoes of it. He had the uneasy feeling that he was being prayed for. He

Elias, the hired man, took Aunt Mary and the children to the train. Little did they realize what a family crisis was in the making from this decision to brave Emil's expressed displeasure at their ten-day absence.

was working as hard as he could work at the college and was making up in the summer for what he had missed in the few months after his mother had died. He had ignored the still small voice so long that it was reasonably quiet now.

After the camp meeting, Emil really "blew up." John was ashamed of him when he heard about it. It all came about when the children had calmly told their father they were full-fledged Seventh-day Adventists now, for they had been baptized at the camp meeting. Fritz had mentioned it first at the supper table on the very evening they had come home. He looked straight at his father when he told of the miracle of baptism.

He knew very well what his father's plans for him were. He was to have the farm, and John and Fred were to have an education.

With his meal only half finished, Emil rose from the table, his face red with wrath. Was it possible that this was the very Emil who had rebelled so at *his* father's tyranny, right on these very acres? Could this be the same person who as a youth could almost feel the chains clank around his ankles? Now he was seeking to bind his son, not in body alone but his soul as well. And the terrible thing about it all was that Emil knew he was actually rebelling because his son had chosen the way of life rather than the way of death. He *knew* he was wrong, yet in spite of it all, he was choked with a blinding black fury, and shoving his chair back, slammed out of the house.

Later on Fritz went to the barn to help with the chores. When Emil saw him coming he almost wished he could die. Fritz's face looked so pure, so good, and so earnest. Words he did not want to speak poured from his lips like black hornets swarming from his mouth, stinging and wounding and hurting. He had not wanted to speak those ugly, hateful things, and he felt sick at heart at the quick, hurt, wounded look the boy cast at him. It reminded him of the look of a tiny fawn he had seen lying by its dead mother's side one cold winter day. This was his Jeanie's boy, and he was shouting at him—not for doing evil but for doing good. Dear God, what was happening to him?

It was queer, but a Bible text came to him. It was doubly queer, for it had been years since he had read the Word of God. But somehow the text seemed like an accusing finger, and it filled him with a sort of terror. It was about Judas and how he had sold himself to do evil. Had he, Emil, also sold himself? Had he so stilled the good inclinations that his love for the lad who looked so much like his Jeanie could not stand before the strong waves of his vindictiveness? He moaned aloud at the sight of the lad's pale sensitive face. Hurrying out of the barn, he did not recall that another man, more righteous and noble than he, had struggled with the same enemy:

"For the good that I would I do not: but the evil which I would not, that I do," said the noble Paul. Later, in contemplating his miserable state, he had cried out in agony, "O wretched man that I am! who shall deliver me from the body of this death?"

If Emil had gone on as the apostle had done and cried for real deliverance from the sins that seemed to rule his life, he might have saved himself a lot of the heartache he would have to endure before he could conquer his stubborn will. Again and again he saw his own father in himself, and he despised himself for having become what he had hated as a young man.

EMIL HAD ENTERTAINED the hope that effects of the camp meeting would die down, but he was dismayed when both May Rachel and Fritz took it into their heads that they wanted to go to the academy rather than to the local high school. Emil, still struggling with himself, refused to help either of them. Strange to say, John turned dead against it, too, and wrote and urged that they stay home and help dad. So it was Aunt Mary, May Rachel, and Fritz against John and Emil. Emil thought if he made it clear that they need not expect any help in a money way, the school idea would be frozen out; but he forgot that Fritz was his son, and had an indomitable will like his own. As he himself had done when he went to Battle Creek, so Fritz took his own destiny in hand. He did not propose to follow the plow and chafe under his chains as his father had done. He would do something about it. The lad got the sales prospectus of *Bible Footlights,* a religious book, and the first thing the family knew, he was out selling it. May Rachel went to stay with a friend of Aunt Mary's, and with another girl was selling a magazine called the *Watchman.* They were having wonderful success, too. Emil was secretly pleased, but was a little too proud to show it, yet he always hung around when the letters came, and he loved to listen as they were read. Mary saw that his opposition was brittle and not real, and realizing that the Spirit of God was working on his heart, she rejoiced.

"They're going to get scholarships, Emil," she said one day, after reading a long enthusiastic letter from Fritz. "I never saw the beat of the courage of those two children. Real go-getters—we can surely be proud."

"Well, they get it honest," Emil said with becoming modesty. "I never let anything lick me. I dug out and fended for myself—I——"

"You surely did, Emil," Aunt Mary praised, glad of his softened mood. "Jeanie always was proud to tell us in her letters of all the things you accomplished."

"Did she?" asked Emil, proud that she would tell

him that. He got out his old work hat to go back to the field. At the door he turned back.

"Tell them I will help them if they need it. We can sell the piano—if——"

"Oh, no, Emil; don't sell that. We want May to play —to take lessons; that would have pleased Jeanie. The hens are doing real well and egg prices stay up. I don't think it will be a bit of trouble." But Aunt Mary sang about her work that afternoon. And while she worked she prayed for the two in the colporteur work, for John in college, and for Emil, who had drifted so far from the religion he must know was right. She sighed as she thought of the old evenings of confidences, when he had seemed so eager to learn all he could. How could he have turned away from it all? Her efforts seemed wasted. But they were not, for nothing is wasted—ever.

JOHN, AT COLLEGE a hundred miles away, was also trying to quiet an uneasy conscience. Surely, he told himself, the whole world cannot be wrong. He had reason to be uneasy and worried. He had a girl friend now, and she was so much in his thoughts he could hardly keep his mind on his studies. His grades were dropping, and he felt bad when Professor Bryant had talked to him for a long time about his lapse in scholarship. Yet when he was with Mollie he forgot all about it and felt the fever in his blood again. What he saw in her he could not, in his sensible moments, explain. She was pretty, so pretty it almost made his head swim, but she was so trifling and irresponsible and downright stupid that he realized he was making a mistake. Yet he was obsessed by her, and chided himself for his lack of judgment. He was risking everything he had aspired to for Mollie, and she was not worth it.

But she was chic, for she dressed well, and was remarkably poised, considering her limitations. When she turned her liquid brown eyes up to his, John forgot that he had determined to make something of his life, and all he could think of was Mollie. She was the daughter of the Reverend Stephen Cartwell, who presided over the vast pile of stone that was the most fashionable church in his college town. Walking past the lovely home next to the church, John told himself that it made no difference what day a person kept as the Sabbath, just so he kept one. He told himself this so often that he fancied he believed it. And he began to take an assiduous interest in the church, attending the services regularly.

He would sit in one of the rear pews, all in a fever, and wait for Mollie to make her appearance. She would come in with a jaunty little coat on, which she wore like an ermine cape. He could tell her little clicking walk without ever turning his head.

One thing that made John uneasy was that someone began to send him *Present Truth,* a little religious periodical. It was either Aunt Mary, or May, or Fritz, and he was afraid it might be his brother or sister, for it was mailed from the academy where they were now happily going to school, for they had both earned their scholarships. He knew nothing of the correspondence bands, and of how Fritz and May would carefully wrap a copy of the little paper and address it to him. But he was sure it was May's vertical handwriting on the wrapper, and it touched his heart a little in spite of himself. Since his talk with Aunt Mary, John had had no appetite for pork, though he had a hard time to explain his refusal when someone offered him a ham sandwich or suggested some sausage and hot cakes. One night at Mollie's house he found himself in a hard situation when the salad she had made with her own dainty hands was full of shredded ham. He had eaten it, but had almost become ill thinking about it.

Then, since Prohibition was in force, some of the fellows thought it smart to carry hip flasks and to drink some of the "hooch" on the sly. He tasted it once and wondered why anyone would get up a temperature over such vile stuff as that; besides, he had, at great inconvenience to himself, gained the victory over cigarettes and was not in the mood to get into bondage to anything else.

One evening John took Mollie to a dance at the Eagles' Hall, over the big drugstore downtown. The hall was crowded, and Mollie's small person was so sleek and dainty that she was the envy of most of the girls who were there. They made snide remarks that John overheard, but he was so infatuated that he could hardly take his eyes off her. He fancied that half the fellows in the hall were envious of him.

Suddenly, right in the midst of the gay rollicking music and the shouts of laughter, and the cigarette smoke that hung like a cloud over everything, a terrible thought came to John. He had been idly reading in the *Present Truth* that had come only that day. He had slit the paper open, and the words leaped out at him, "Jesus is coming! Are you ready?" What if He should come while he was here! The thought seized him with such violence that he could not hear the idle patter of conversation that Mollie was making.

"What's the matter, Johnny? You look funny. Don't tell me you're sick—you look pale."

"I—I guess I don't feel so good. Let's go out and get some ice cream." But she had not wanted to go—no, not at all, and somehow John found himself out in the air— and he realized that she was not going to miss him a whit. He was out of sight and out of mind as far as she was concerned, and suddenly he knew he was healed of his obsession for her.

The examinations were held that week, and as soon as he knew he had passed with honors, he was out and gone. So cured was he of his infatuation that he wanted never to see Mollie and her vacuous pretty face, or hear her silly titter any more. But there was one thing that hurried him more than anything else. And that was the memory of the time when he had said something about his folks' being Seventh-day Adventists, and Mollie had laughed and laughed until he was thoroughly angry.

*A*T HOME DAD had little to offer him, and he wondered whether he would ever find any work to do. Dad let him work in the dairy and paid him, but it was not what he had prepared himself to do. Of course, that was not unusual. A lot of his schoolmates had had to take what they could. One had trained to be an accountant and was now clerking in a grocery store. Another had studied law and was now working in a soft-drink bottling works. It was discouraging. Times were hard, and there seemed to be no opening for a young fellow all primed to face the world and to make a niche for himself.

He avoided Aunt Mary for a number of reasons. For one thing, he was condemned because he had a secret feeling that she was as right as rain, and he was not of a mind to make his position any more complicated, as he was afraid taking a stand for truth would do. And another reason was that he felt sure she had more truth for him, and he wanted none of it. He had enough to face as it was, and he did not see how he could handle any more. So reasoned John very foolishly, as if truth were a liability and error an asset. But that is as Satan would have us think.

So for a few weeks John only marked time, until one day Emil came to him with a newspaper, all excited over an advertisement for a farm in Saskatchewan. He was of a mind to send John to see what was what about the place. If there was money there, as some people seemed to think, then he would sell out here and make the move. The big house was a worry to him since Jeanie was gone. The report in the paper told of all the wonderful produce that could be grown on the land there, and so John soon found himself on the train heading west toward the Canadian farm in which his father was interested. He had never traveled much, and the ride on the train was a great treat to the nineteen-year-old boy. He was at the window looking out all the time, and when they came to big cities he got out of the train, so curious and eager was he.

$\mathfrak{B}$UT THE FARM was not what it had been written up to be. Emil would never be happy here, John was sure, for he had been told how much colder it got than in the old home, so he wrote dad accordingly.

"This is a pretty country; you would like that part of it, I am sure. There are great forests, and a belt that is wonderful, they say, for agriculture. They have a lot of cold weather up here, much colder than at home; and that is why I think you might not like it. There is one section down in the southwestern part that lies within the area affected by the chinook winds, and they say that cattle can be pastured there the year around; but it sounds funny to me. The farm you wanted me to see is not what they described it to be, and you would not want it."

He went on and told his father that he wanted to stay around and see the country, but would be back in a few weeks. He had found a place to stay with a farmer, and one morning the farmer asked him what education he had, and what was the chance of his teaching in the district school.

John was startled at this, yet he asked to think the thing over, for he had not earned a dime for some time and his bank account could bear a little replenishing. Times were so hard that even family men were working for two and three dollars a day. He learned on inquiry that he would receive the sum of ninety dollars a month, besides the free rent of the "teacherage," a house that had been provided for the one who taught the school. Of course, he realized he would have to be janitor as well as teacher, but that was not unusual. So he accepted and wrote home accordingly. To his surprise he found that he was allowed a sum of money for food and coal in addition to his salary, and he felt rich. He determined to save all he could of the money he earned.

ONE COULD HARDLY have found a more isolated place. The nearest town was twenty miles away, and the mail came from twenty miles in the other direction. Fifty-five pupils of Russian-German origin crowded his schoolroom, and if he did not get fat, it was no fault of the kind mothers of the settlements.

"Mutter says she baked, and here is some brot," one would say, handing John a huge loaf, like as not accompanied by a roll of homemade butter.

"Apple strudel," another would laconically say, putting a carefully wrapped bundle on teacher's desk. He ate well and seldom had to do any cooking. And because he had heard the German language all his life, as well as English, it was not hard to fit into the niche of the country school. He was a great favorite. He had his violin and he

172

taught the whole school to sing as they had never been taught before. In fact, John was a little surprised at himself, for the emergency brought out the realization that he was gifted musically. He might never have found it out, but in teaching the children to sing he found a deeper pleasure than he had known. People came for miles around in farm wagons to attend his "exhibitions" and his singing schools. At noontime the schoolhouse was odorous of sauerkraut and black rye bread.

When he went out to visit the parents they sometimes prevailed upon him to stay all night, and he would stay and from books he had read tell stories to the heart-hungry prairie folks. Everyone from the old grandmother with her flashing knitting needles to the child on his mother's lap would listen with rapt attention. Then he would sleep, like as not, under a Russian feather quilt, with another just like it under him. No sheets, no blankets. John smiled when he thought how aghast Mother Jeanie would have been at such a sleeping arrangement. At least it was warm.

He liked that year so well that he went to the government college at Regina for summer school. He taught again the next year, all the time increasing his savings in the bank. Then he took a school in a small town, and because he thought it was good business policy, he began going to church. It was not long before he was asked to teach a Sunday school class. Things went along fine, without any unpleasant incidents, till it was almost time for school to be out the next year. One week the Sunday school lesson was on the Ten Commandments, and John studied the lesson through carefully. Not satisfied with his preparation, he rummaged through his trunk for a book the hired man had given him several years before. It was *Bible Readings for the Home Circle*. Gus had assured him that "every single livin' and abidin' verse in the Scriptur' was there, and no mistake, and mebbe some besides that." He had "never seen sich a book," but he wasn't much of a reader, and if John was a mind to, he could have it, and welcome. John had taken it, and now he got it out to see how it came about that the Ten Commandments were done away with, as so many people told him. He was determined to know when and why.

He learned very quickly that it is still a sin to steal and kill, and to be impure and unholy and idolatrous. And he learned by an overwhelming array of scriptures that the Sabbath still stands, as do the other commandments, and will stand until the redeemed go into the new earth, where the Sabbath will still be kept. He read in Isaiah 66 that the saints of God will gather to worship the Lord "from one new moon to another, and from one sabbath to another." The next Sunday John taught that the commandments are still binding on Christians. One of the boys spoke up, laughingly, and said, "Well, one of those commandments is not binding, and I know that for a fact. My father said that that was proof that the commandments were for the Jews and not for Christians to keep."

John looked up quickly and noted that it was the minister's son who had made the sage observation. He smiled at the boy and asked him which commandment was it that he thought was a good thing to break. But the boy hastened to observe that he had no mind to break any, unless it was the one about keeping the old Jewish Sabbath holy —who on earth would think of keeping Saturday, of all days!

"My mother did," John replied, surprising even himself.

"She did?" several of the boys exclaimed in unison. "Are you a Jew, Mr. Huener?"

"No, I am not a Jew, nor was she," he answered slowly. "But I have never found any place in the Bible where the Sabbath was changed from the seventh to the first day of the week, and I wish someone would tell me why we keep Sunday in place of Saturday. I would really like to know."

"Why don't you ask your mother?" ventured one.

"She is dead," replied John, not caring to reveal that she had been untrue to what she believed for many years.

A day or so later the minister came to John's rooms to see him. After a few casual observations, the subject of the previous Sunday's lesson was brought up, and Reverend Packer told John that he had had many complaints from the parents about the way he had handled the lesson on the Ten Commandments.

"I am sure you did not mean to lead the young people astray, Brother Huener," he said affably and apologetically. "But when you told them that you did not know why the Jewish Sabbath was not kept today, it roused a regular hornet's nest. My phone has been ringing all week."

"I cannot understand that," John said, his dignity a bit affronted. "I said nothing but the truth, and I feel sure it is the truth. I do not think there is a place in the Bible where it tells that the Sabbath was changed to Sunday. When the boys asked me, or mentioned it, I could only tell the truth."

"It is not always a good policy to be outspoken, especially on mooted subjects," the minister said soothingly. "But I told them that you were young and did not realize that you were stirring up the boys and making trouble for me and the parents, too."

"Why trouble for you?"

"Listen, lad, I am the one who has to meet these things, and let me tell you there is no issue in the Bible that is harder to meet than that one, for it can be as difficult as the Gordian knot."

"You mean you have no explanation of the fact that you keep Sunday when the Bible expressly commands the keeping of Saturday?"

"Of course Saturday is the right day, and anyone would be foolish to deny it. It would simply show his ignorance of sacred and secular history. The Seventh-day Adventists have all the proof on their side, and if I was a stickler for the letter of the Scriptures I would be bound to be one; but I am not, and I for one do not believe God is that particular. I don't think it makes a bit of difference what day we keep, just so we keep one."

"Then why, precisely, are you taking me to task for wondering whether we should keep Saturday? If it makes no difference to you, why can't I keep Saturday and you keep Sunday, and the rest of the town keep Wednesday if they want to? Why should you worry if it makes no difference?"

"B-b-b-but it does—here in this town. The parents won't stand for their children to be confused and mixed up, and I must ask you to let me get another teacher for the class you have been teaching."

Seeing that the minister was becoming angry, John saw the futility of further argument. He recalled an old saying his mother was so fond of:

"A man convinced against his will
    Is of the same opinion still."

"Thank you," he said to the minister. "I will not come to church any more."

"Oh, don't feel that way," the man said lamely, as he picked up his hat to go. "I am sorry to have to tell you this, for the boys have been very fond of you. It will upset them, but——"

"Tell them I am going back to where my father lives," John put in. "That ought to clear you, for school is out this week anyway."

ISGUSTED AND DISHEARTENED with the way his life was turning out, John took the train East, hoping against hope that something would break pretty soon for him in the line of work in which he was interested. He had not been well for some weeks, and he thought to go to the old family doctor in his home town for a checkup. He was so ill sometimes that he could hardly get through the day. Thinking that perhaps he needed a tonic, he bought several patent remedies in the drugstores, only to find that he was worse off both financially and physically.

At home Aunt Mary gave him one look and put him to bed.

"John, you hadn't even ought to be walking around. Up to bed with you, and I will take your temperature. Emil, you call the doctor."

John was so dizzy he could hardly get his clothes off. Big as he was, he did not mind when he felt Aunt Mary's cool, capable hands helping him in his fumbling efforts. He managed to put on a clean nightshirt and crawl between the clean cool sheets, although it seemed as if the whole room was revolving slowly about him. He must have blacked out for a while, but he soon was wakened by the doctor looking him over.

"He has an infection somewhere, and I wouldn't be surprised if it was his appendix. We'd better get him to the hospital."

From then on John's life was one plateau of pain after another, and one agony more exquisite than the last. He was burning, he was freezing. He was so nauseated that he was afraid he would die, and then he cared not if he did. His tongue felt like a hard cob in his blistered mouth, and his back and legs ached intolerably. Dimly he was aware of Emil's coming to see him; of Aunt Mary's presence. He was aware of their speaking to him and of his utter inability to answer or to make a sign that he understood. Indeed, he did not understand too well. Just a little.

One day he overheard the doctor and the nurse talking by the bedside. He had become a bit more alert mentally, but seemingly worse physically.

"Poor fellow, I think he's done for," the doctor said. The word pricked John like a thorn.

"It is a shame," the nurse answered. "He is well educated and had a bright future. When do you think he will go?"

"He will not last the night out," the doctor told her.

"He hasn't known a thing for more than a week, and he hasn't taken any nourishment."

"Too bad," she replied, as she took his pulse and noted his respiration on the chart. "Are you sure he doesn't understand?"

"Not a chance. He is like a log."

Then they went away, and John was more awake than he had been for days. So he was going to die. These were the last hours of his life. It was unthinkable. He opened his eyes and looked around. There was a glass of ice water on the table. Suddenly he wanted that worse than he had ever wanted anything in his life. He tried with all his strength to lift his hand to get it. It was within reach, but he could hardly get his hand off the bedcover more than an inch. Suddenly it became the prime object of his life to lift his hand. He approached it from every angle. He strained his eyes to look down at his hand. He saw it fluttering upward. His heart soared with joy. He could—he could—he could—he could lift his hand. Now, just a little this way—right there was the table—that way —ah—his hand was touching the glass—his fingers were closing around it. Now to pull it—easy now—let it sit till he could raise his head. Now to raise his head—up, up— now the glass—not spill—just a sip—to put out the fire that burned his lips, his tongue, and his mouth——

He wondered afterward how he ever achieved it. The nurse came in later with another nurse.

"I was sure," she said, "that I filled that glass with ice water. I was sure, and it's only half full now." She looked at John speculatively. "I wonder——" she said. Then she was gone. He took another drink while she was gone, emboldened by his former success, but for some queer reason he wanted to keep the fact from her. Then, suddenly, he thought of his life. He thought of his dreams of being a great man. He thought of what his mother had told him in one of her rare talkative moods before she had died. She had told him that she had dedicated him when he was only a babe to be a minister. John pondered it all. She had been a Seventh-day Adventist when he was born, and that meant that mother had wanted him to be a Seventh-day Adventist minister. A kind of wonder filled his heart.

Life seemed very precious to John, now that it was apparently ebbing away. Then conscience came alive, and he thought of some of the mean things he had done; of how he must have wounded his mother's dear heart when she was ill and weak and facing the dark alone. He had been strong and had not known what it meant to be ill and helpless and near the waters of the dark river.

Oh, if he could only live. If he only could. If he just could live—even one more day. Painfully he turned his head. It was dark outside. He could hear cars down on the street—and voices. There were people out there, and they were living. Why were they not shouting for joy that they could live! His breaths were numbered—only a few more. Oh, what he would not do if he had life.

He tried to think of the good reasons he had summed up for not keeping the Sabbath, and for turning away from dear Aunt Mary when she had come in and healed the breach in their home and in the hearts of his brothers and sister. What would they do without her? Slowly he turned his head. Someone was coming into the room. It was dad. Poor dad. He was crying. He wished he could say something to dad—but—— And there was Aunt Mary, her eyes red and sad. They knew. They had been told that he was going to die, and tonight. Why couldn't he tell them—but what would he tell them? After a while they turned away. John decided to get another drink. It took a long time, but he did, and strangely, no one saw him. Then he heard father talking in the hall. His voice was broken—he was sobbing. Great, harsh, tearing sobs.

"You go home, Mary," he was saying. "We can't do anything now. It is all over. I will have them phone you——"

"Yes, Emil, there is something I can do," he heard Aunt Mary say. "I can pray. I have seen them raised up in Battle Creek when——" And then John was not able to hear the rest of what she said, for they must have been walking down the hallway. His heart swelled with the thought. She was going home to *pray* for him. To *pray* for him to live. Why, he could live if—if he asked in faith, believing, for he had heard folks say many times that if a person had the faith of a grain of mustard seed he could remove a mountain. He turned his head slightly. There on the bureau was the luminous dial of a tiny clock that was presumably put there by his nurse. It was 1:30—one-thirty on Thursday morning, the sixteenth of July. It must be the sixteenth. It must be Thursday, for he recalled that someone said the evening before that it was Wednesday the fifteenth. Funny how things of such little consequence stick in a fellow's mind. Why couldn't he speak? Maybe he could if he tried, as he did when he put his hand up. Now, get ready, fix your mouth. Say, "Dear God, help me," and pray for the grain of mustard seed. No, no, not that—no—pray for faith—pray for faith——

Oh, he was trying so hard. He concentrated all his will on his mouth. Now say—say, "Dear—dear." Out of the silence he heard his own voice. It said, "Dear"—just perfectly. He was working hard to frame his words. Did everyone in the world have to work hard to pray? God, do You see me? I want to pray and I can't. I want life—dear God, and if You give me life, I will give it back to You. I will—I will. I can see so many things plainly now. They are so plain, and things are right at the level of their worth now—just what they are worth. Some things I used to treasure are not worth a thing. Other things I took for granted are worth a king's ransom—God, God, God, —give me the mustard seed—no—faith——

Suddenly he awoke. He must have dropped off while he was praying. He looked up. The sun was streaming into the room, and the breeze lifted the curtains. Dad and Aunt Mary and the nurse and the doctor were by the bed.

"I never saw anything like it, Mr. Huener," the doctor said. "He took a turn for the better right after midnight. I was in and out of here all night, and so was Miss Glasgow. She said she never saw a patient sleep better, and he must have taken a whole glass of water, though how he did it, she can't fathom."

"I did," John said, looking up at them. "I did."

"He's better, Emil," Aunt Mary wept. "Oh, Emil, he is going to live."

John looked at them.

"Yes, I am," he said slowly and carefully, measuring every word. "I prayed—I told God I would follow Him—I will—too."

$\mathscr{J}$OHN WAS BAPTIZED at the campground that year, and even Emil was present. They had all prayed that he too might return, but he did not seem to be ready, though everyone knew his heart was touched. Then John went to teach another school out on the prairie, about fifty miles from home. It too was a big school, and the whole community seemed to revolve about him. It was common knowledge that he was a Sabbathkeeper, and some of the people tried at first to engage him in argument, but they were so confuted by the pleasant, clipped way he had of clinching everything with a Bible verse that they marveled at his scriptural knowledge. It engendered in them a reluctant but wary respect. The superintendent of education knew what John's religious faith was and told him he figured it was nobody's business as long as he taught the school all week. This he did. But when his students were curious and began asking him questions, he was hard put to know what to do. He loved the Bible and all its lovely truths, and yet he wanted to sidestep trouble all he could. So he told them to go and read their Bibles and see if they could come up with the right answer. You never saw so many young people reading the Bible as there were that year.

At the same time John led the community in music, singing, and clean social times. Everyone liked him, and some few tried to "convert" him.

One day Grandma Stivers, who was an inveterate matchmaker and who had tried to introduce him to any number of "nice girls," told him, "Mr. Huener, there is the prettiest girl who has your religion right here in this very county. And listen here, she is as smart as a whip. Do you know, she is a returned missionary from Iceland? And her so young, too. She went there to convert the heathen."

John laughed at that.

"Grandma, there are no heathen in Iceland."

But Grandma was not to be contradicted. "They ain't Methodists, and that is just the same," she said. "But let me tell you, she is as smart as a whip. I heard her recite several times at meetin's, and I will tell you she can make you believe you are right there where she is talkin' about."

$\mathcal{J}$OHN HAD BOUGHT a model-T Ford sedan, and he was now able to go to church each Sabbath. Curious about the young woman whom Grandma had described to him, he discovered she was all that the old woman had said, and more. When he heard that she was going to finish college, and already had her application in, John was so excited that he sent his application in the next day.

How could he describe Virginia Payson? Gray eyes, alert and full of understanding. A pretty oval face that had strength in it, yet softened by a laughing red mouth. Her swift, capable hands only accented the grace and poise of all her movements. He lost no time in meeting her and was in a frenzy of fear lest she should not like him, but when he asked her to go with him to hear the great Alexander Graham Bell, the inventor of the telephone, she accepted without hesitation.

"Oh, Mr. Huener," she cried with great delight, "I am

so glad to get to go. I read of his appearing in Capital City, but I did not see how I could get there, for I do not have a car. May we take someone else with us—too?" And then John saw the modesty and decency of her—not wanting to be out alone with him late at night, and he appreciated her all the more.

"I will be glad to take your mother or your sister or anyone you would like to have go," he told her.

The upshot of it all was that her mother and father did go with them, and they had a fine evening together. They were well pleased when they found out that John was attending the same college that their daughter was. May Rachel went too, and so did Fritz. Little Fred was old enough now to go to the academy, and Emil was helping! He was as proud of his children as he could be. And so the years fairly flew by.

It was a few days before graduation when a message came to John. It was in a long white envelope, and he opened it curiously. Inside was the call to an island mission field, a place where the need was great and where a school was to be established. From the school would grow other institutions. Who knew?—it could be a hospital or a publishing house or a college. It must be the beginning of great things. If he were married—— Was he contemplating marriage soon? To what kind of girl? Would she be adapted to life in a primitive country? How was their health? et cetera, et cetera, et cetera.

"I want you to go with me, Virginia. We can be missionaries together—
that is, if you trust me. I love you so, for you are all I have ever dreamed
of. I can do the work of the Lord all the better with you at my side."

John got up and paced the floor, his heart full to the bursting point. Oh, if Mother Jeanie had only lived! Then she could have seen that her dearest dreams were coming true. Then he stopped short. He would have to take this letter and show it to Virginia, and ask her whether she would go with him to that faraway island field. She ought to be willing—she had already been to Iceland. When he saw her, he turned as bashful as a schoolboy. He could hardly bear to say a word for fear she might say she did not feel she would fit into his life plan. He felt that he would die if she should say this. He found her darting out of the dormitory on the way to the bookstore. However, she was not in such a hurry but that she could stop and read his letter. Then when she looked up he managed to blurt it out—what he wanted her to know. She looked at him appraisingly, frankly, in the way he had liked. Not silly, vacuous, and speculative, like some of the girls he had known, but sweet and dear and businesslike. Here was someone he could always depend on—that he knew.

"You say, John, you want me to——"

"I want you to—to—go with me—Virginia. We can be missionaries together. That is, if you trust me—if you think you can. I love you so. You are all I have ever dreamed of, and I believe I can do the work of the Lord all the better with you at my side, helping me. Can you—do you——" He floundered, looking at her with pleading eyes.

SHE STOPPED a moment and looked across the beautiful campus. There was an old sundial set in the midst of an oblong island in the sidewalk. They were standing near it. She looked at him, a serious expression in her sweet eyes.

"I guess I have thought a lot of you, John," she answered. "I wondered many times whether you cared about me."

"And I was afraid to ask you until I had something to offer you," he put in eagerly. "I wanted to prove myself—to make good. Will you trust your life with me?"

Her gray eyes grew serious.

"Trust you? Ah, yes, John. I can trust you, for you know and love God, and you have pledged your life to His service. There is no finer measure of integrity than that."

The day after graduation there was a simple wedding in the chapel. Aunt Mary, Emil, May Rachel, Fritz, and Fred were there. And Virginia's mother and father and sister worked all that day to get her belongings packed. Aunt Mary and Emil helped too. Help was needed and quickly, for John and Virginia were to spend their honeymoon on the high seas—sailing toward the sunrise, and toward a more abundant life.